TEN PISCATAQUA
WRITERS
2026

Ten Piscataqua

Paperback Writer Series
Ten Piscataqua Writers 2022
Ten Piscataqua Writers 2024
Ten Piscataqua Writers 2026

Studio to Coffee Table Book Series
Ten Piscataqua Photographers
Ten Piscataqua Painters

TEN PISCATAQUA
WRITERS
2026

An Anthology from the Watershed

Edited by

Phillip Augusta

James Patrick Kelly

Mary Ann Cappiello

& Richard Foerster

Ten Piscataqua · PO Box 1354 · Portsmouth, NH 03802 · *www.tenpiscataqua.com*

Some of the works in this anthology have been previously published.

James Gatto's "Clara Beller and Larry Andrews" first appeared in *Once Upon a Happily Ever After Volume 2* (Independently published, 2024).

Abbie Kiefer's poems first appeared in the following periodicals: "Our Neighbors in February, 63 Degrees with No Clouds" (*Sweet Tree Review*, 2019); "The Possibility of Loss" (*Naugatuck River Review*, 2019); "Certainty" (*Booth*, 2020); "A Brief History of Yankee Thrift, Yankee Ingenuity, and Yankee Work Ethic" (*Sixth Finch*, 2023); "Better Home, Better Gardens" (*Electric Lit*, 2024); "Heliotropism" (*New Letters*, 2024); "It's June Now" (*The Cortland Review*, 2024); "I've Learned to Accept" (*Bracken*, 2024); "My Hundred-Year Flood" (*The Missouri Review*, 2024); "On *The Early Show*, Martha Stewart Explains How to Keep a Home" (*The Account*, 2024); "On *House Hunters*, the Buyers Always Insist They'll Need Space for Entertaining" (*The Journal*, 2024). "A Brief History of Yankee Thrift, Yankee Ingenuity, and Yankee Work Ethic," "Certainty," "It's June Now," and "I've Learned to Accept" *Certain Shelter* (June Road Press, 2024).

Jason Allard's short fiction "Some Kind of Hero" first appeared in *Live Free or Dragons* (Plaidswede Press, 2019). "Shugyosha" first appeared in *Compass Points: Stories from Seacoast Authors* (Piscataqua Press, 2015).

John Perrault's poems originally appeared in the following publications: "Hill, Milton & Wright" (*The Main Street Rag*, 2024); "Early Morning Rain" (*Innisfree Poetry Journal*, 2024); "For the Birds" (*Constellations*, 2022); "The Piano" (*The Ballad of Louis Wagner*, Peter Randall, Publisher, 2003); "The Conversation," "I Like It" (*Here Comes the Old Man Now*, Oyster River Press, 2005); "The Blue Hood," "The Times" (*The Comstock Review*, 2017 & 2007); "Up on the Border" (*The Aurorean*, 2020); "In the Laurentians," "Northern Point" (*Résonance*, 2024); "Poem Beginning with a Line by Tomas Tranströmer," "Connoisseur" (*Orbis*, U.K., 2015 & 2021); "Buddy Bolden" (*Naugatuck River Review*, 2019); "Foreclosure" (*The New Verse News*, 2012); "Bag Lady, Christmas Eve, Manchester, NH" (*Grey Sparrow Journal*, 2023); "Emilio's" (*Burningwood Literary Journal*, 2023); "My Neighbor" (*Hole in the Head Review*, 2021); "Whatever You Got Going On" (*Rock and Root*, Rock Weed CD, 2013).

Bob Gielow's "The Culling" first appeared online at <u>creepypasta.com</u> (Creepy Pasta, 2015).

Paul Goodwin's collection of poems first appeared in his book *Preliminary Findings* (Bee Monk Press, 2024).

Madeline Kearin's short story "Witch Hole Pond" first appeared in *Litro Magazine*, 2020.

$25.00
ISBN 978-1-7379723-3-4

Ten Piscataqua
PO Box 1354
Portsmouth, NH 03802-1354
www.tenpiscataqua.com

Set in Minion
Book design by Phillip Augusta
Cover painting by Steven Henry Lee

Table of Contents

About the Writers

James Gatto

I began writing fiction six years ago. Although I now live in Exeter, I spent most of my life teaching theater arts, both performance and technical, in north-central Connecticut. My first writing venture was entitled "Frenchtown" which I described as a "semi-fictional memoir." I wrote it in novel form, and also scripted it for voice actors so that it could be recorded as a podcast. All major podcast platforms carry it. My second venture was a fictional biography/short story collection entitled *Once Upon a Happily Ever After Volume 1*. The story contained herein, "Clara Beller and Larry Andrews," is from *Once Upon a Happily Ever After Volume 2*.

Peter Welch

My chapter includes excerpts from the boyhood memoir I'm currently writing, *I Kiss the Ground: Boyhood, Belonging and the Kinship of Nature*. The story's action takes place where I grew up in Moody, Maine, during the 1960s and '70s. I explore the labyrinth of my boyhood life through proximity to other boys and men as

I unearth a sense of belonging, both within my own being and through the small town world I inhabit.

In May 2024, at sixty-three, I completed an MFA in Creative Nonfiction Writing at Bay Path University. So far, my writing can be found in *River Teeth Journal* and *Multiplicity Magazine*.

Along with writing, I'm also a watercolor painter. As a cog in the animal transport wheel, I occasionally drive rescued southern dogs to new northern homes. I've met extraordinary people here, primarily women, who care about other sentient beings like I do. I volunteer at the Kittery Freebie Barn and am struck by our human push and pull of material possessions. The natural world is both balm and muse in my life, and trees are some of my most revered teachers and companions. I live in Kittery Point, Maine with my partner Michael and our sweet (rescued) pup Dasher. To learn more about me or my work, check out at my website: *peterwelch@weebly.com*.

I'm grateful to Ten Piscataqua for inclusion in this anthology and for a unique opportunity to celebrate local writers.

Abbie Kiefer

In my work, as many writers do, I keep returning to my preoccupations. My chapter in this anthology includes poems from two separate projects, my first book and a book I'm still writing, but the pieces feel connected because they are—all of them threaded through with the concerns that hold me: legacy and belonging and my desire for permanence in an impermanent world.

My work is also influenced by geography and regional identity. Save for a little time spent in the South, I've been a New Englander all my life—in Maine until my mid-20s and then in Seacoast New Hampshire for the last 15 years. I'm the author of *Certain Shelter*, a collection published by June Road Press in 2024. My poems have appeared in *Copper Nickel*, *Gulf Coast*, *Ploughshares*, *Prairie Schooner*, *The Southern Review*, and other places. If you'd like to learn more or contact me, please visit my website: *abbiekieferpoet.com*.

Jason Allard

I'm an Army brat who grew up all across the US and saw much of western Europe during our three years in West Germany before settling here after graduating from UNH in 2000. My family's been in the Piscataqua watershed since the 1690s and in New England in general since the Mayflower.

I started trying to write stories as far back as first grade. I toyed with it some through high school and while earning a BA in English from UNH. By far, I learned the most about writing from my time at the Odyssey Writers' Workshop, and the annual The Never-Ending Odyssey workshops for Odyssey grads. Much of my writing is in the area of speculative fiction (Sci-fi, Fantasy, and Horror), inspired by growing up with the tales of King Arthur and Robin Hood while being able to look out my bedroom window and see two actual castles on the horizon. So far, I have about twenty short story sales.

I've done many jobs since leaving school, including nighttime Circulation Desk at UNH's Dimond Library, and now I'm a machinist at Portsmouth Naval Shipyard. I'm also a self-taught bladesmith thanks to the power of YouTube and inherited blacksmithing tools.

I currently live in Kittery with my librarian wife, Amanda, and our three rats, Sokka, Juliet, and Raven.

John Perrault

I landed in the Watershed in 1966 to teach English at Traip Academy. Ten years sharing poems with students sharing their lives with me in return. Learned more from them than they did from me. Week-ends all music—gigging with Mike Rogers—he on the blues harp, me on guitar. A year of graduate study tucked in there somewhere. Then three years of law school, thirty years of practice. (Practice makes perfect they say.). All the while, writing songs, poems, recording, playing the occasional gig. I read some-where you know who you are when you learn what you can't do without. Sounds about right. So I wrote. So I write. Publish in the journals when I'm lucky. Nine albums, three books and a chapbook so far. What about?

The winds must come from somewhere Auden says. My early poems unfurled out of songs. These poems—grouped in threes—focus on what out there happened to be blowing my way, hitting my head. My heart. Any moment something hard knocking at the door, shaking the house, making me cuss; something soft, light as a leaf, making me smile: Bones. Beach stones. Birdsong. Ballads. Can't seem to turn around without taking on the world. I'm upset. Excited. Delighted. Appalled. Angry for being angry. Happy when giving thanks. Theme, if any: Follow the rock and root path. Pick up a pen, a brush, a lute, a lens. No or yes? Lean toward the latter.

Bob Gielow

I have been a college administrator for over thirty years, authoring emails, sending letters of accep-tance to applicants, editing policies, and setting up various forms for my applicants and students to use. When I caught the fiction-writing bug, a dozen years ago, I found that epistolary formats, such as email exchanges or text messages, offered a terrific way for me to spin tales that were clinical and thorough in describing my characters, their thinking, and actions; all without diminishing my ability to explore the resulting human emotions. When I figured that out, I was off to the races writing stories as diary entries, a newspaper advertise-ment, an obituary, a course description, local newspaper articles, a corporate message to patrons, a press release, a retirement speech, and Wikipedia posts. Although I don't always use non-traditional formats in my story writing, I am usually creating stories that I wish were real, in some fashion. I invite you to read my stuff to see what I mean. I have over 40 short stories published in numerous online and print publications, such as *Paragraph Planet,*

101 Words, Door = Jar, Maudlin House, Short Kid Stories, Gorko Gazette, Dark Horses Magazine, Every Day Fiction, Heimat Review, and *miniMAG Literary.*

Matt Miller

I was born and raised in Lowell, Massachusetts where early on I had the Kerouacian dream of being a holy goof football player poet. After graduating from Lowell High School, I went on to Yale, but poetry was scarier than football, so I mostly stuck to the athlete script until a neck injury in my senior year landed me back in the library, scribbling poems and stories in the stacks. After college I worked as a landscaper and security guard and then went to Emerson College to get an MFA in Creative Writing. Around the same time, I fell in love and eventually married a Lowell girl, Emily Meehan. We started a family with our first child, Delaney. Not long after, we moved from New England to California after I received a Stegner Fellowship in Poetry from Stanford, where I studied with the great Irish poet Eavan Boland. Family and work called us back East though, and we ended up in Exeter where our son Joseph was born. I teach English and coach football at Phillips Exeter Academy and have published several collections of poetry including the award-winning *Club Icarus* and *Tender the River.* When I'm not teaching or writing, I'm surfing the New Hampshire coastline. Lately, I have been working on personal essays. The two pieces in this collection are part of a larger collection of essays I am writing about fatherhood, teaching, and tender masculinity. You can find out more about my work at *mattwmiller.com* and contact me at mattwmiller89@gmail.com.

Jane C. Elkin

I am a word nerd who gets to play with language every day while teaching English to immigrants, an experience detailed in my 2014 chapbook, *World Class: Poems Inspired by the E.S.L. Classroom*

(Baltimore: Apprentice House). With a B.A. in English from Bates College and an M.F.A. in creative nonfiction from Bennington Writing Seminars, I discovered my authorial voice when my musical one first betrayed me in 2007, thus changing my creative career path from that of classical singer to freelance essayist and reviewer for *The Bay Weekly* in Annapolis, Maryland. Since then, my poetry and prose have earned awards from the likes of *The Old Farmer's Almanac,* The Poetry Society of New Hampshire, and The Maryland Writers' Association, and appeared in such markets as *Popula.com, The Best of Ducts.com,* and *Ruminate.*

The wife of a former naval officer, I have visited all fifty states and most of western Europe. I practice my French, Spanish, and Polish daily and knit blankets while binge-watching historical dramas. Though my Google Nest is tuned to acoustic rock and classical vocal stations, the loudest thing is my house is generally the hum of the fridge. To learn more, visit *www.jcelkin.net.*

Paul Goodwin

When I left college teaching back in the '80s, I had spent 32 years in classrooms (including a year learning Chinese in the Army) including graduate school studying rhetorical criticism. From then until my retirement at the end of 2018, I made my living as a writer, including five years as writer/editor of Trivial Pursuit, five more as an information designer and many years writing a guide to investing in Chinese stocks. Although I've always been drawn to poetry, it took the Portsmouth Poet Laureate Program to really get me into the poetry habit. I haven't studied poetry under anyone, taken a poetry class or published any poems outside the Piscataqua watershed. When a friend introduced me to PPLP, Hoot nights (first Wednesdays of the non-summer months) I was hooked by the camaraderie and love of poetry that suffused the group. Eventually, I joined the Board and served as Chair for two years. Outside the PPLP, my Seacoast New Hampshire profile depended more on my film critic gig with *re:Ports.* magazine and my 25 years leading film discussions at The Music Hall. After my wife's death after years of Alzheimer's, I collected my poems and published them with Bee Monk Press in a volume entitled *Preliminary Findings.* My poetry has always been motivated by the open mic at PPLP Hoots and odes and celebrations for friends' occasions. The poetry I like most is at its best when it's read aloud, and that's how I recommend appreciating mine. Need a reader? Give me a call!

Madeline Kearin

As a writer, I'm interested in anxiety. I like writing about characters who have been driven by fear to inhabit small, cramped quarters, but are forced by circumstance to reengage with the world. Their stories might play out in dramatic, earth-shaking ways, or—in the case of Molly in my story "Witch Hole Pond"—entirely within their own heads. I am less interested in what *really* happened than in how it tests and transforms the protagonist. My writing is also informed by my experiences as an archaeologist, exploring the lives of people in the past from the material traces they left behind. I graduated from Sarah Lawrence College and earned a PhD from Brown University. From 2013-2014, I directed the excavation of a Revolutionary War site in my hometown of Mount Kisco, New York. My next project was the Worcester State Hospital for the Insane in Massachusetts, which I studied while working in the archives of the Worcester Historical Museum. My book on the topic, *A Refuge of Cure or Care,* was published in 2021.

My fiction has appeared in *Conjunctions, Prairie Schooner, BFS Horizons, Beloit Fiction Journal,* and *Litro.* My story "Mytholmroyd" was the winner of *Prairie Schooner's* Bernice Slote Award for best work by an emerging writer in 2020. I live with my husband and two daughters in Kittery.

About the Crew

Phillip Augusta • Editor

I began publishing photo postcards of the region in the late '70s, one of which became that "Portsmouth" tugboat-in-the-fog poster you used to see everywhere. Soon after came *re:Ports.*, an arts and entertainment weekly calendar that grew to become a voice for the regional music, writing, and arts communities in the early and mid-'80s, just when fine restaurants and live music venues were rebranding Portsmouth's military town image into more of an upscale cultural hotspot. An arts weekly was really about discovering and promoting local talent—live music in the seven-column calendar centerfold for the fridge, with visual artists on the cover and local writers of fiction, nonfiction, and poetry inside as the pages grew. I've since worn a variety of creative and production hats in the book industry, and editing the Ten Piscataqua books today is again about finding a sustainable way for the community to discover its homegrown talent.

James Patrick Kelly • Fiction Editor

Although I grew up in the suburbs of NYC, I atoned for my upbringing by moving to New Hampshire in 1976, the year after I sold my first story. I've been on the Seacoast for the past thirty-four years.

At this point my writing scorecard features six novels, over a hundred and sixty stories, a dozen or so plays, a handful of poems, and twenty-seven years of my regular column "On The Net" for *Asimov's Science Fiction Magazine*. I write mostly science fiction and fantasy and have won several of the genre's awards. The short fiction has been reprinted in many Year's Best anthologies and overseas in fifteen different languages. Among the other accomplishments of my checkered past are fifteen years teaching at the Stonecoast Creative Writing MFA program and eight years serving as a councilor on the New Hampshire State Council on the Arts.

Mary Ann Cappiello • Nonfiction Editor

Nonfiction literature has long been a passion of mine. As a Professor of Language and Literacy at Lesley University in Cambridge, Massachusetts, I teach courses in children's and young adult literature and literacy methods, including a specialized course in nonfiction for children and young adults. Prior to that, I served as a curriculum facilitator for English Language Arts and Social Studies at the middle level, and taught middle and high school English Language Arts, Humanities, and creative writing in New York and New Hampshire. I'm lucky to have many opportunities to collaborate with other literacy educators and scholars of children's literature; I am coauthor of *Reading with Purpose: Selecting and Using Children's Literature for Inquiry and Engagement* (Teachers College Press, 2024), *Text Sets in Action: Pathways Through Content Area Literacy* (Stenhouse, 2021), as well as *Teaching with Text Sets* (Shell, 2013) and *Teaching to Complexity: A Framework for Evaluating Literary and Content-Area Texts* (Shell, 2015), and my work has also appeared in *Bookbird: A Journal of International Children's Literature, The Reading Teacher, English Journal, Language Arts, The Dragon Lode, School Library Journal,* and *School Library Connection.* A founding member and contributor to The Biography Clearinghouse, I have also reviewed children's and middle grade books for NCTE's *Language Arts* and chaired NCTE's Orbis Pictus Award for Outstanding Nonfiction (K-8) Committee. My debut young adult biography will be published in Spring 2027 with Holiday House.

Richard Foerster • Poetry Editor

I grew up in the Bronx, the son of German immigrants, and earned degrees in English literature from Fordham and the University of Virginia. My first book, *Sudden Harbor*, appeared when I was 43 and has been followed by eight others: *Patterns of Descent* (1993), *Trillium* (1998), *Double Going* (2002), *The Burning of Troy* (2006), *Penetralia* (2011), *River Road* (2015), *Boy on a Doorstep: New and Selected Poems* (2019), and *With Little Light and Sometimes None at All* (Littoral Books, 2023).

Over the years I've been fortunate to have several honors come my way, including the "Discovery"/*The Nation* Award, *Poetry* magazine's Bess Hokin Prize, a Maine Arts Commission Fellowship, the Amy Lowell Poetry Travelling Scholarship (which allowed me to travel around the world for a year), and two National Endowment for the Arts Poetry Fellowships—as well as two Maine Literary Awards for Poetry. Since the late 1970s, my poems have appeared widely in magazines and anthologies, including *The Best American Poetry*, *Kenyon Review*, *TriQuarterly*, *The Gettysburg Review*, *Boulevard*, and *The Southern Review*.

Stints at artist retreats have nourished my work—at MacDowell, the Virginia Center for the Creative Arts, Yaddo, Hawthornden Castle (Scotland), the Camargo Foundation (France), Fundación Valparaíso (Spain), Cimilece Castle (Czech Republic), the Tasmanian Writers' Centre (Australia), La Napoule Arts Foundation (France), among several others.

When I was not persuing the next poem, I worked at various times as a lexicographer, educational writer, freelance typesetter, and editor of the literary magazines *Chelsea* and *Chautauqua Literary Journal*. Now mostly retired, I live in a former Nazarene church in Eliot, Maine, with my partner, the artist Douglas Taylor.

Linn Schulz • Copyeditor

Bit by the writing bug in Milwaukee before I reached my teens, I started with poetry in third grade but my voracious reading, besides getting me in trouble with my parents, sucked me into an obsession with words and language. Bullshit my way into my first job as paste-up artist and editor (sole writer) of a Time Insurance home office magazine at 18, my career segued into typesetting and eventually to preventing my clients from embarrassing themselves in print. Sharing my life in New Hampshire with musician Tom Hall, traditional English folksongs became the soundtrack of my life. I became godmother to the Portsmouth Maritime Folk Festival, session regular and, after Tom died, She Who Must Be Obeyed of the weekly Anglo-Celtic Press Room session. I live in a quirky house in the Nottingham woods surrounded by stacks of books and ephemera, and bullied by an orange felinity named Rufus.

Lynn Davey • Website Admin

I have worked as a creative for over nineteen years in a variety of industries, including print shops, a local newspaper, a signage company, and an upscale home and garden magazine. I ultimately found my home as the owner of LD Creative Designs, a marketing agency based in Newfields, New Hampshire.

I am passionate about the conservation of land and spend a lot of my free time roaming around local trails or hiking mountains in the North Country. I am also a proponent of animal rights and welfare.

Steven Henry Lee ◆ Cover Artist

I have been working as an artist in the NH Seacoast since receiving a BA from the University of North Dakota in 1974. I work in both 2D and 3D, in design, and construction. Presently I am concentrating on painting, graphic design, and a limited number of sculpture projects. I worked as a decorative artist with Mural Works where we completed numerous public art projects (1985–1995), and as an educator teaching mold making for sculptors. I have also worked in building design and construction specializing in masonry as the primary building material.

My 3D skills are in clay modeling, casting, and mold making. In 2D, I paint in oils and acrylic, and draw figuratively. I pay attention to the harmonious interplay between the elements in the composition and I prefer to let the medium suggest the subject rather than emphatically describe it. Most of my work is intuitive, albeit disciplined and evolving.

I operate a studio where the Dodge Avenue Drawing Association (DADA) has been holding weekly drawing and painting sessions since 2014. We are a small group dedicated to the study of the human form. My work can be seen at *www.dada-studio.net*

James Gatto

Clara Beller and Larry Andrews

This quietly affecting story appears in a longer work called, Once Upon a Happily Ever After Volume Two. *The premise is that you, the reader, are visiting the Ruttledge Village Cemetery in North Central Vermont and the cemetery's caretaker, Lester Bacchus, acts as your guide to the graves and regales you with stories about the dead. Sometimes, as in this piece, the dead speak directly and eloquently. The story starts and ends with Lester's comments.* JPK

Lester

Clara Beller is buried here and Larry Andrews is over there. You'll notice that Clara passed on October 30, 2017 at the age of 60, and Larry passed on the same day having just turned 10. This isn't a coincidence, as you'll soon see.

If you travel west along High Street, pass the fire station, and continue on about a half mile, you'll see a depression on the right side of the road. It's set far enough back that it will appear as little more than a rectangular, shallow hole to anyone traveling by car. There's a story that's attached to that cellar hole. On the surface, it's a tale about how people who don't choose to conform to the norm sometimes open themselves up to become the objects of misunderstanding, suspicion, even superstition, by those who live more conventional lives. Clara Beller was one of those nonconformists, not by dress, behavior, or reputation, mind you, but only by geography, as she and her husband, Roger, had originally chosen to farm land outside of Ruttledge's neighborhoods and its commercial and cultural centers. In some eyes, especially ones young enough to be called innocent by many, ignorant by a few, this marked Clara as a recluse, a hermit, an apostate, and, around Halloween time, a witch. Don't be surprised by this. I think it's fair to say that every generation singles someone out to be a witch as that spooky time of year approaches, a time when the harvests have been brought in, leaving the fields to weathered scarecrows that seem to almost hover above ground-hugging seas of mist that arise out of nothing as darkness sets in.

This story is also about how unintended consequences can sometimes change lives and fortunes for the better, and sometimes not.

I'll let Clara Beller tell you about how she and Larry Andrews first met.

Clara

If we had a witch in Ruttledge back when I was a youngster, I don't remember her. Of course, Halloween wasn't as popular in those days as it is now. I remember that an article in the *Reader's Digest* said that it was becoming almost as big a money-maker as Christmas. That article stayed with me mostly because it was in my first *Reader's Digest* large print issue that came in the mail. I had to subscribe when it became too much a burden to walk all that way into town to read the library copy.

Roger, that's my husband, bless his soul, had these big plans for buying up all the surrounding farmland. He was going to grow vegetables for Ruttledge and neighboring towns, and breed cattle and pigs for local butchers as well as for the meat departments of village markets. He even wanted to buy sapling fruit trees to start an orchard. That's why he moved us out here when we married. Land was cheap back then, but, even back then, labor wasn't. We were overwhelmed by the work. We struggled to keep up even though we worked from sunup to sundown, seven days a week. Most of the local population either had to tend to their own crops, or got work at the John Deere Tractor Assembly Plant, once it opened, over in Rochester. Roger had hoped that high school-age kids would want to earn some spending money during their summer vacations, but those few who signed on weren't reliable, especially when the town authorized the Academy to add a new wing which housed an indoor swimming pool.

Larry

We never set out to hurt that old lady. Honest to true, we didn't. We was only barely in fourth grade, and it was comin' on to Halloween. That art lady, who came to our class twice a week, she had us all riled up with drawings of pumpkins and ghosts and witches on broomsticks with black cats. Then, the tenth graders put on a play about them Salem witch trials. This one girl, Melinda Bateson her name was, she accused an old lady of bein' a witch. She was a witness, and when a lawyer asked her to show what the old lady done, then she went all wild-like, crawling on the floor, and screechin' somethin' terrible. Everybody was scare't. Some, second-graders I think, started to cry and their teacher, Mrs. Davis, had to take them outa the auditorium. I used to have a crush on Mrs. Davis when I was in second grade, but now I got a crush on Beverly Alexander, one of my sister's friends.

Anyway, the next day, on the playground, one of the third-graders said he heard that we had a real witch in town. Her name was Old Lady Beller, and she lived outside a town cuz everybody was afraid of her, and nobody wanted to live near her. That's what he said. Somebody else, another third-grader, I think, said that she had all these black cats, and mixed up spells in a big black pot. A girl said that she heard that the old witch lady caught spiders and then ate 'em like candy. Everybody made that "euwww" gross noise.

That Saturday, me and my friends, Tommy and Robert, rode our bikes way out there. We weren't supposed to go that far, but we pinky-sweared not to tell anybody. We found the place easy enough. There was an old lady hoeing in a garden out in back, but we figured she couldn't be the witch because she wasn't dressed in black, but then my friend Robert said that maybe she "transformed" into a witch after dark, like that girl in the play that started out normal and then turned into a demon or something. The house looked normal: maybe kinda run down. There were pumpkins on the porch steps and dried cornstalk bundles tied to the beams holdin' up the porch. We didn't want to get any closer. Besides, we were afraid that, sooner or later, somebody'd drive by and see us, and then tell our parents where we were. So, we started back home.

Clara

Roger passed without warning just after he turned 60—way too young. He had complained about being extra tired, but it was harvesting season, so I put it down to longer than usual days in the garden. He went to sleep one night, and he was gone in the morning. Never made a sound, at least as far as I could tell. We were sleeping separate back then, on account of his snoring, which got worse over the years.

Loretta Leete made the drive out in the hearse personal to take Roger in her care. Awful nice of her to do that, I thought. I drove to the parlor later that day to tell her what I could afford, and to fill out some paperwork that the coroner would require. Loretta said that she'd contact Ralph Patterson, who drove the Golden Age Bus to tell him to add me to his route, but I told her not to bother. I had the old Dodge for grocery shopping and doctor appointments. She said she'd tell him anyway, because I might need transportation if the weather was bad. Then I was off to the cemetery to talk to Paul Gourlie, our local mason, about a gravestone and the inscription. Roger had bought a plot for four soon after we married. That was in case we had kids, which we never did.

It was really hard to walk into the house for a while. It was so quiet that I took to leaving the kitchen radio on all day, even when I had to go out. At least that way there'd be some noise goin' all the time, so I'd never come home to complete silence. I even tuned it to what Roger used to call a "kid station," because at least the music was lively. Sometimes, if I went up to bed early, I'd forget to turn the radio off, but I got used to sleeping right through it, so that were no never mind.

Larry

I don't remember who had the idea of visiting the old witch's house on Cabbage Night. In case you're unfamiliar, Cabbage Night is the night before Halloween. My pa told me that Halloween used to be about makin' mischief, like smashing pumpkins on the road or knockin' on people's doors and then running to hide, especially if the people inside chose not to "treat" you, that is. He said that's where "trick or treat" comes from. In other words, if you give me candy, I won't play a trick on you. But now, my dad said that me and my friends only wanted to collect as much candy on Halloween as we could carry, so nobody played tricks on Halloween anymore. Instead, now they played the tricks the night before, Cabbage Night.

One of the big kids told my sister that him and his buddies use to collect dog poop for Cabbage Night and put it in paper bags. Then they'd leave it on somebody's front steps, light it on fire, ring the doorbell, and run and hide. Then, when the owner opened his door, he'd stomp on the bag to put out the flames and end up with dog poop all over his shoes. That sounded like a real fun adventure, so me and my friends, Robert and Tommy, decided to try it out on the old witch on the next Cabbage Night.

Clara

My sister, Eloise, tried to talk me and Roger into adopting. I was open to finding out more, but Roger was dead set against it. His argument was always "we can't afford a family." The topic rose to the surface every few years, until it eventually changed to "we're too old to start a family." And, by then, we were. So, we went about our daily routines, just us two. We had to work hard every day to keep the farm going, but we weren't exactly scratching a living out of it either. We paid our taxes and our electricity bills on time just like anybody else. When we needed new clothes, we bought them. We traded in our old car for new every five years, always a Dodge, nicer than a Plymouth, but cheaper than a Chrysler. And we always took two weeks at the shore. We went into town every Friday to get the "Early Birds Menu" at the Ruttledge House. Roger always had meatloaf; I always had the fish special.

I don't think that either of us took into account the toll that age would take until Father Time began to knock on our door. We were lucky, I suppose, that neither of us suffered a medical calamity or developed the sort of health condition that often comes with growing older. On the other hand, because we lived dependable, healthy lives (good diet, regular exercise, plenty of fresh air, etc.), we didn't recognize the compromises to aging that we were gradually making. I'm thinking here, for example, of how we began hiring some temporary help to make sowing in the spring and harvesting in the fall a bit easier. Or how Roger's occasional late afternoon nap in his favorite chair, eventually became too frequent to be called "occasional." As for me, I used to go upstairs at 10:00, then 9:30, now 9:00, and sometimes even earlier. We even began skipping our weekly Friday visits to Rut-tledge House because it was too cold, or too hot, or raining, or just because we couldn't be bothered to change out of our work clothes. Those are the kinds of compromises I mean.

One night we saw a program about how the world's population was growing larger and larger. The show's host was saying that it seemed ironic that people living in the poorest countries continued to have the largest families. He said that countries like India, for instance, also have the poorest medical systems, which means that many children die as infants or in early childhood. As a result, parents keep makin' babies because they want to have enough children to take care of them when they get too old to care for themselves.

That program really brought home to us, I should say "to me," how the choices we make in our youth can come back to haunt us in what are supposed to be our "golden years." If we couldn't afford to have someone come in regular, and given that we could never afford residential care, who was going to help us when the time came that we couldn't fend for ourselves? My first thought was to call around to some ladies I know so that I can gather some information. I mean, I don't even know the difference between Medicare and Medicaid! There is a difference, isn't there?

Larry

First, we had to collect dog poop. I didn't grow up with dogs, so I couldn't offer any help. My friend Robert had a chihuahua named Chico, but its poops were too small. Tommy, my other friend, had a cocker spaniel named Muffin. Its poops were bigger, but still no cigar. We were almost gettin' desperate when Robert volunteered his neighbor's dog, Ranger, a big German shepherd. His poops would be perfect, but how were we going to get them? Robert said we should ask permission, but I said that sounded pretty weird. I mean, what do we do, knock on the door and say, "Can we please collect your dog's poop?" Then Tommy said that we could explain that we needed it for a science project, but that sounded even weirder. Then I said that maybe we could say that we wanted it to fertilize our garden. But who ever heard of using dog poop to grow vegetables? Cow poop and horse poop, yeah, but not dog poop. We were stuck. But then Tommy said we should just steal it. We liked that idea a lot because it would keep us feelin' like this was a real adventure.

We figured that Robert could knock on his neighbor's door and say like he was selling magazines for school. Robert's dad saved all his old *Field and Stream* magazines because, according to Robert, he liked to look at pictures of fish, and we always had old *TV Guides* kicking around our house (on account of my ma liked doin' the crosswords), so we could borrow a few to use for examples. Then, while Robert's neighbor was distracted, Tommy and me would scoop the poop. That was the plan.

We tried it on Saturday morning. Robert went to the front door, while Tommy and me hid in the woods behind his neighbor's house. We had an old plastic beach bucket and spade that we found in Robert's garage. Ranger, the dog, was inside so the coast was clear. When we heard talking out front, me and Tommy ran into the backyard and started scouting for poop. We found it right away, four or five piles, but they were old turds, and everybody knows that when turds get old they get hard, and hard turds wouldn't be any good because they wouldn't smush when somebody stomped on them. We kept lookin', but we just couldn't find any fresh poop. Just about then, we heard Robert startin' to whistle. That was the signal we worked out for him to tell us to scram. So, me and Tommy ran back into the woods poopless.

We regrouped in Robert's garage a few minutes later. He couldn't get over that we hadn't found any. He thought maybe Ranger might be sick or somethin'. So, we decided that the best thing was for us to hide in the woods and spy on Ranger. Then, when he took a fresh dump, we'd grab it quick and wrap it in plastic so it wouldn't dry out on account of Cabbage Night was still two days away. So, we went from pooper scoopers to pooper snoopers. Turns out the reason that Ranger hadn't produced any soft turds was because he was what my granma called "regular" and it wasn't his usual time yet. I mean, we couldn't have been the woods for a half hour, when Ranger was let out and went straight into a squat to take an awesome dump. I mean, he must have been savin' it for some special occasion or somethin'. As soon as he was let in and the back door closed, we raced into the yard to snag it. We let Robert have the honor because it was his beach bucket and spade.

When we got back into his garage, we transferred it into a plastic grocery bag and closed it up tight with one of then twisty things. And didn't it just stink. It was perfect! We then worked out a plan for Cabbage Night. I came up with the idea of tellin' our parents that we were goin' to Susan Ludlow's Halloween Eve party, which was a real thing that she had every year on Cabbage Night. She lived over on Elm Street which was just far enough for us to want our bikes to get there and back. So, the plan was to meet in front of The Academy at 7:00 and leave from there. That would leave us enough time to "trick" the old witch and come back to Susan's party while it was still going on.

Clara

I never bothered to buy any Halloween candy because I was too far out of town for any kids to bother. The Golden Age Club had a Halloween party for seniors at the Grange Hall from 8-10. A friend of mine, Enid Hawkins, invited me to join her and some friends who were going. I was tempted 'til she mentioned that people were bein' encouraged to wear costumes, and there would be music and prizes. Abner and me went one year dressed like that old farmer couple in the famous painting, but turns out two other couples had the same idea. Besides, Lorne and Martha Turkell won that year. They were Tweedle Dum and Tweedle Dee—you know, from "Alice in Wonderland," that Disney cartoon. It was a natural choice for them, because they were both pretty round even without the costumes. The year before they came as a pair of blueberries. They each wore a sheet, dyed dark blue, with a hole cut out for their heads, and a green, feathery hat that Martha made. They didn't win that year, but, from then on, nobody called them The Turkells anymore; everybody in town referred to them as "The Blueberries." Sounded better than "The Turkells" anyway. So, I told Enid that it was too soon for me to be out in public cuz I was still in mourning, and she accepted that.

Actually, Roger passed at a convenient time—for me anyhow. I hope you won't think poorly of me for sayin' that, but it was true, because of the farm, I mean. We'd just about finished harvesting fall vegetables and were pretty well stocked for the winter months. The last thing we did before the cold weather set in was to put the garden to bed, meaning that we spread horse manure on it, and worked it in with iron rakes, then spread straw over the top. That usually took a couple of dry days. We had just finished dinner, when Roger said something about feeling more tired than usual and headed up early. Next morning, he didn't come down for breakfast, and he didn't answer when I called, so I went up to check on him, and he was already cold—must've passed as soon as he got into bed.

The funny thing was that I just came back downstairs and had my breakfast even before I called Loretta. I didn't feel anything right off. It didn't seem real somehow, like I was dreamin', but I knew I wasn't. I cleaned up my breakfast things and left Roger's eggs and bacon on the table for him, while I went out to feed the chickens. Then I walked over to the field and finished spreading the hay on it where Roger had left off. He'd left his rake right there in the garden, leanin' 'gainst the scarecrow, so I used that. Then I came in and called Loretta. Then I sat at the table staring at Roger's eggs.

Larry

We met at the corner of Elm and Main just liked we planned. It had been lookin' to rain all day, but it had stayed dry. Some folks said we was in a drought, but you wouldn't think that from lookin' at those clouds. The reason I'm bringin' this up is so you'll know that it started getting dark earlier than usual. We was all excited, like you'd expect. Robert had emptied the Ranger poop into a paper bag. He said that it had stayed nice and soft, and boy was it ripe. He double bagged it, but that didn't seem to help the smell much. Tommy volunteered to carry it.

About halfway to the witch's house, Tommy said, "wait a minute" and suddenly braked. I figured he was chickening out, but then he said, "Who brought the matches?" Robert said, "That wasn't my job, I handled the poop." Tommy and me looked at each other. We both knew we didn't have to ask each other. Then I said, "I'll ride back and get some; we'll still have time," and I started to turn my bike around, but then Robert said, "No, you can't. We'll be ridin' home in the dark!" He was right of course. So, the three of us just stood there straddlin' our bikes for what seemed like a long time. Then, I said, "Hold on I got an idea. Did you and Tommy bring flashlights?" "I did," Robert said. Tommy said, "Yeah, I got mine, "and I said, "me, too. So, before we give up and start back, let's drive on a bit, checkin' the sides of the road for those little plastic lighters that everybody uses. As soon as they start to run out of gas, people throw them out their car windows and buy a new one. There gotta be some between here and the witch's house. We just need to find one with a little gas left cuz we're just gonna use it once." Robert said, "That's a great idea!" And Tommy said, "Yeah, good thinkin'. You guys check on this side of the road, and I'll check over on the other side."

So, Tommy crossed over and we, me and Robert, pedaled just fast enough to not lose balance, whiles't all the time we was aiming our flashlights at the ground. Before too long, Tommy yelled, "I got one, guys!" all excited like. Me and Robert crossed the road to where Larry was. He was holdin' it up like a gold medal, but when he held it up to his flashlight it looked empty. "Ain't there supposed to be liquid in there?" I asked. Robert said, "Yeah, my sister carries one, but there might still be a little. Try it." Tommy did, the little wheel on top sparked, and then a tiny blue flame flickered, but it only lasted a second or two and then it went out. Then Tommy flicked it again, and it sparked again, but this time there wasn't any flame. He tried a few more times, but it was the same, sparks but no flame. "That's okay," Robert said, "Let's just keep lookin'. There's gotta be more." So, me and Robert crossed back to our side and we started searchin' again. I said to Robert, "You know, this feels like a real adventure, don't it?" I felt kinda silly sayin' it at first, but then Robert said, "Sure does," and I didn't feel so embarrassed.

I used to daydream about goin' on real adventures. Sometimes I was in a jungle, trying to rescue my secret crush, Beverly Alexander, a seventh-grader, when she was tied to a tree and surrounded by all these snarling lions and tigers. Other times, I was in the Old West and she was tied to a cactus and all these Indians were aiming their bows and arrows at her. And sometimes I was in outer space, and she was captured by alien lizard men and they had her strapped to a table in their mother ship, and they were all grouped around wearing white aprons and getting ready to perform horrible experiments on her. Meanwhile, I was always running, riding, or zooming in with my rocket jet pack to rescue her. And I always did. A few times, I even had dream adventures like that, and they were so real that I hated when I woke up.

This one, the flaming bag of dog poop adventure, wasn't anywhere near as good as my dream ones, but, just as I was thinkin' that, my flashlight reflected off of something red and shiny. "Hey, guys," I yelled. "I think I got one!" As I was bending to pick it up, Robert pulled up next to me, and Tommy raced from across the road. Sure enough, it was a red one, and, when I put my flashlight behind it, we could all see liquid. It was almost a quarter full! Tommy said, "Let's go!" But I said, "Wait, let me make sure it works first, because maybe the sparky thing is broken." Robert said, "Yeah, try it first." So, I did, and it lit up right away, and the flame was bright and steady. So then, we all whooped and hollered and set off again. And this time, it really did feel like an adventure again.

Clara

I was the only one seated in the family chairs next to Roger's coffin. His parents were long gone, and his older brother hadn't been heard from in years—not even a Christmas card. He was dead, too, for all anybody knew. My parents had both passed, and I was an only child, so I was the only person to keep a vigil over Roger's earthly remains. Plenty of people came to pay their respects. In fact, I was surprised to see that Roger had so many friends, though, to be honest, many of them were more my friends than his. Roger didn't make friends easy. He mostly kept to himself, and to me. Anyhow, we had the wake and the graveside service. The stone that Paul Gourlie carved was real nice.

It wasn't until after a couple of weeks had passed, and I'd gone through all of Roger's things, and I'd donated his clothes, the few worth donating, that it really started to hit home. Loretta Leete, bless her heart, called about then just to see how I was getting on, and I told her what I just told you. She said that I might talk to Reverend Simms, who conducted Roger's service, but I told her that me and Roger weren't regular about goin' to church, so I'd feel kind of embarrassed about asking him for help now. She said she understood because she only went herself on the holy holidays like Christmas and Easter.

Then she said something that's stuck with me ever since. She said that maybe I was in a state of shock on account of how Roger was taken so sudden, and now it was startin' to wear off. And I said that I'd admit that the first week or two with the wake and the funeral and the clearin' out of Roger's stuff didn't feel real somehow, but I was over it now. But Loretta said that some people are in shock for weeks; they just don't realize it. She said that people, like me, who've lost loved ones, especially "life partners" (that's what she called Roger and me) can't properly mourn and start healin' until the shock well and truly wears off. Then she asked me a question that was pretty personal. She said, "Do you find that you're cryin' more now than you were before?" I swear, I nearly jumped outta my chair. "Yes," I said. "I didn't cry at all those first few days. I was even fake crying at the wake and the funeral. I mean I tried, but the tears just wouldn't come. But now, I cry 2 or 3 times a day, and I mean I cry a flood, not just a trickle." And Loretta said, "That might prove my point. But you think on it. And think about calling Reverend Simms, or even Doc O'Connor. Or call me, I'm no expert, but I'm always prepared to listen. Meanwhile, think on this: when the shock wears off, the mourning starts, and, when the mourning ends, the healing begins." So, I thanked her very much. And she was right of course. The healing did begin, but so did the worrying. Was I going to be able to stay here? I couldn't begin to manage the farm on my own. Me and Roger had barely been able to keep it goin' with two of us workin' all day every day. Winter was a quiet time, so I knew I had a few months to sort everything out, but the thought of spring kept me awake more than a few nights.

Larry

It was just beginnin' to get on to dark when we spotted the house up ahead. Up until then only a couple of cars had passed us, each goin' in the same direction as us. Each time we saw a car comin' we quick pulled off the road and hid behind whatever bushes were close by, so we felt pretty safe about not bein' spotted by someone from town. There was a clump of trees just short of the house, so we got off our bikes and hid them there. Then we took the bag of dog poop, and we stoop-ran up to the near side of the house. We could see that there was nobody outside, and it was too cold for anybody to be sittin' on the porch, but there was lights on inside on both floors. Then Robert whispered, "Who's gonna plant the poop and light it?" I said, "It's your poop, you plant it." Tommy said, "Hang on, why should you get all the glory? I wanna be able to tell the big kids that I did it too." "Yeah," I said, "that's good thinkin'. I wanna be able to say that I was more than just a lookout." Then I says, "Okay, how's this? Robert hid the bag in his garage, but Tommy carried it all the way from town. How about if Robert carries it up to the porch, Tommy puts it on the front step, and I light it." We all agreed that was a fair plan. We took one last look to make sure no cars were comin', and then we headed out.

Clara

My last day on earth was typical of what my routine had become after I accepted that Roger was well and truly gone. As Loretta said, the mourning had ended, and the healing had started. I rose at the usual time, had breakfast and thought that I'd spend some time on my knitting, some on my reading, some on my crosswords, and some on my current jigsaw puzzle. First, though, I had to feed the chickens and the pigs. There wasn't really anything left to do outside in the garden except pick a few of the larger pumpkins and place them on the front steps. I knew I wouldn't get trick-or-treaters out here, which was just as well because I hadn't bought any candy, but I figured that I should make a little bit of an effort for people drivin' by.

While I was in the garden, I noticed that some cornstalks were still standing, and I remembered seein' on TV how some people bundled them together and used them as decorations. So, I thought, "That's a good idea," so I got some clippers and a ball of twine from in the barn, and I cut the ones still standin' and tied them into two clumps. Good thing I did this in the garden, too, because the stalks was so dry they would of made a mess on the porch. I tied them to the posts that supported the porch roof. Then I went inside and found some orange ribbon in my ribbon bin and made a bow for each bundle. I couldn't, for the life of me, remember why I'd gotten orange ribbon. It must have been sittin' in the bin for an age—just lucky, I guess. Then I stood back to admire my handiwork. It was pretty good, too. My friends would probably have called it "festive."

Larry

I sneaked up to the porch first, followed by Robert, and then Tommy. I know that my heart was dancin' in my chest, and I'm sure that Tommy and Robert were feelin' the same. I was even startin' to sweat, and it was cold outside. We tiptoed up on to the porch and crossed to the front door. I was a little surprised that Robert didn't just leave the bag on the steps, but I didn't say nothin' about it—wish now I had. We could hear music comin' from inside, so we knew that the old witch had a TV or a radio goin'. That made us feel a little safer, but we was careful to not make any noise anyway, because you had to be real quiet in an adventure. So, Robert handed the bag off to Tommy, who put it on the porch right in front of the door, and then I pulled the lighter out of my pocket and flicked it. At first it just sparked, but it didn't catch fire, so I flicked it again, and still nothin' happened. Then I looked at Robert and Tommy because I didn't know what to do if it didn't work. So, Robert whispered, "try it again, but harder this time." So, I flicked it a couple more times, but still nothin. So, then Tommy whispered, "Bring it here. Let me see it." We ran back to the clump of trees where we started. I said, "Who's got a flashlight?" Robert said, "I do," and he fished around in his jacket pocket for it. When he took it out, we shielded its light with our hands, and he shined it on the lighter. We seen the problem right away. Some lint from my jacket pocket had gotten clogged in the lighter's gas hole. Tommy plucked it out as best he could. Then I tried it again. This time it sparked and then it lit. So, we went back to the porch. Tommy and Robert stopped on the porch steps this time, while I tiptoed over to the bag and lit it. It caught right away. Tommy yelled "Run!" and all three of us took off as fast as we could back to our bikes. We was almost to the clump of trees when Robert yelled, "Stop! We forget to ring the bell!" He was right of course, so all three of us then ran back to the house as fast as we could. The bag was burnin' pretty good by then, so I mashed my thumb on the bell button, while Robert and Tommy both knocked real loud. Then, just like before, we ran back to where we stashed the bikes. I think we ran even faster this time.

Clara

I was upstairs changing into my nightie, thinkin' that I'd come back down to watch some TV and maybe even pour myself a sherry when I heard the front doorbell. "Who could that be at this hour?" I thought, but then I realized that, while it was getting dark earlier now, it had only just gone seven. So, I pulled my dressing gown on over my nightie, slipped into my slippers, and started down, wondering if it was somebody who got lost and needed directions or something like that. Just to be safe, I went into the parlor and pulled the curtain aside a little to spy who was on the porch. I didn't see nobody, but there was a light comin' from somewhere on the porch, so I crossed to the door and opened it. Lord Almighty! It was a fire! It was on the porch floor right on top of the welcome mat. I couldn't see what was burnin' but it gave off a lot of smoke, and it sure smelled foul. My first thought was to stomp on it to put it out, but I was only wearin' my slippers, so instead I decided it'd be safer to kick it out to the steps and then onto the grass. Then I'd go into the kitchen, and I'd get some water and douse it. So, I kicked it good. It, whatever it was, sent up a fair shower of sparks, slid across the porch, and bumped up against one of the cornstalk bundles.

Larry

Me and Robert and Larry were hiding in the trees where we left our bikes, all excited like, when the old witch opened the door. As soon as she yelled, all three of us started in to laughin'. Then Tommy yelled "Liar, liar, pants on fire," and we laughed even harder. Then Tommy yelled it again, and this time me and Robert joined in. So, all three of us was yellin' "Liar, liar, pants on fire" as loud as we could. It's funny how sometimes you'll do somethin' like that when whoever you're yellin' it at won't be able to know who's doin' the yellin' or where the yellin's comin' from. You know what I mean? Just then we seen the old witch kick the bag, and we laughed harder still, because we figured that now her shoes were covered in dog poop, which was the whole idea. But then we seen that one of the corn things had caught fire, so we stopped yellin' and laughin'.

Clara

I started forward to finish kicking the burning thing off the porch and onto the grass, but I could see right off that the corn bundle had started to burn. My first thought was to make for the kitchen and get some water, so I turned to go back in, but then I said to myself, "hang on a minute. I knowed where I tied the bundles to the posts in just a couple of places, so can't I just break the twine or untie the knots and throw the bundle onto the lawn?" Then I thought, "but that twine is strong. I don't know if I can just break it with just my hands, and the nearest scissors are in my upstairs sewing basket." Then I thought, "Okay, if I'm not strong enough to break the twine, and the fire won't let me get to the knots to untie them, then I can still pull out the stalks from between the ties and throw them on the grass. It'll be messier, but it'll still work." By the time I made up my mind, a good part of the bundle was burnin', and I was starting to panic because I could see the flames workin' their way up toward the porch ceiling. So, I forced myself to get near enough to the bundle to see where I might be able to grab the stalks in places that hadn't caught and pull them out.

I hadn't counted on the heat. It was horrible hot. No sooner did I get close enough to reach my hands out than I pulled them back in. It was like sticking your hands in a nest full of hornets. Just then I realized that I should have followed my first instinct to get water from the kitchen, but now even that might be too late. I'd just about made up my mind that I'd have to call the fire department, when those same hornets started to sting my lower legs and ankles. I looked down to see that my dressing gown was on fire. It was about then that I started screaming for help, all's the while knowing that there wasn't nobody close enough to hear me. That's when the real panic took over.

Larry

We saw the old witch tryin' to pull the cornstalks loose, but she was just makin' things worse because every time she pulled at the bundle, a big shower of sparks went up. The wind blew some of them into the other bundle, and we could see that it was startin' to catch too. I yelled to her, "Leave it! Call for help!" and we thought she glanced over at us, but then she just kept pullin'. Tommy and Robert joined in yellin' too, because we could see that her nightgown was startin' to burn down at the bottom. She must've seen it, too, because then her cries for "help" turned into screams. We didn't know what to do. Robert said, "We gotta help her." I said, "Yeah, but how?" Right then, I broke cover and ran toward the porch.

Clara

Once I realized that I was on fire, everything became a slide-show, like the ones me and Roger used to have years ago when there wasn't anything worth watching on TV. He'd set up the screen, I'd run the projector, and we'd watch something like our 25th anniversary party. First, you'd see our friends arriving, then you'd see me and Roger opening gifts, then next picture would show Roger and his friends sitting on the porch drinking beers, then you'd see everybody lined up, paper plates in hand, at the buffet table. That's the only way I can describe it, like I was seeing myself from outside myself, like in a series of pictures.

In my first slide, I see myself stepped away from the cornstalk bundle, looking down at my burning nightie. In the next, I see me bending over, trying to slap out the flames. The next slide shows me still bent over, but now I'm looking up because the flames from both bundles have worked their way up to the porch roof, which is already burning hard and fast. From the look on my face, I seem to be saying to myself "How come it's spreading so fast?"

Then, there's a slide of me looking out front, and the light from the flames shows a boy running right toward me. "Who is he?" Next, it shows him on the porch, and he's using his jacket to try to knock down the flames. I'm standing off to the side, and my nightie is burning even more now. I look like I'm in a kind of trance, because I'm watching him instead of trying to put it out. The next slide shows that his jacket is burning, too, so he dropped it. Meanwhile the whole porch is filling with black smoke. In the next photo he's grabbed my hand and is trying to pull me off the porch into the front yard, but the whole space between the bundles is now a wall of smoke and fire. Just then, the next slide shows me looking off to the left because I think I hear other people yelling, "not this way, the other way!" The next photo shows the boy pulling open the screen door and dragging me inside. "Who are these people? What are they doing here? Why don't the others help, too?" In the next slide, we're inside and he's grabbed a blanket off the couch and he's throwing it over me to snuff out the flames. Meanwhile, the thick, black smoke from the porch is now fast filling up the front room.

Now, I know you're dying to know what I was feeling right then, I mean, how could I stand the pain, right? Truth is, there was no pain; I don't know for sure when that happened, but it did. And I was grateful for it. Roger lost the tip of his left middle finger to a table saw before I met him, and he said the same, that it was only painful right when it happened, not after. He said that he asked the doc about it while doc was stitching him up, and the doc said that he was in shock, and that nature designed it that way so's we'd stay awake, because otherwise, if the pain was too great, we'd faint, and, if we were alone, we could bleed out before anybody could find us. But, and this is a big "but", while I couldn't feel nothing, I could still see, hear, and, worst of all, smell. Do you know what burning flesh smells like? When it's your own burned flesh? I smelled like an overdone pork roast. Just then he yelled, "Where's the kitchen?" I tried to speak but nothing came out, so I raised my hand and pointed. It was right then, that I started to realize how bad off I was, because the arm I was looking at was all black and red, and I couldn't open my hand to point because my fingers had fused into my fist.

He stepped behind me and steered me by my shoulders into the kitchen and over to the sink. Then he turned on the water, and sprayed me head to toe with the spray-thing that I use when I wash my hair. Meanwhile, the radio was playing a happy tune.

Tommy

Me and Robert barely saw Larry drag the old witch into the house on account of all the smoke. The whole porch was on fire by then. Robert said, "I'm goin' to ride to the fire station to get help. You stay here and flag down anybody who drives by." I said, "I'll come with you," and started to mount my bike, but Robert was already pullin' away by then. He looked back over his shoulder and said, "Stay and see if there's a hose." I dropped my bike and sprinted over to the side of the house, staying well away from the front because it was burnin' fierce now. A little tree halfway up the front path was even startin' to smoke.

Sure enough, there was a water spigot behind a bush on the near side of the house, but it didn't have a hose attached. I was only half surprised because my dad always said they had to take our hoses in when it started frosting, because, otherwise, the water inside would freeze, and then the hose would burst. I tried to look in a window, but the curtains were drawn tight, so I decided to check the back of the house, hoping that the witch might've left a hose attached back there, but there wasn't one. I went up the back steps and pulled open the screen. The back door was locked, and there was a curtain behind its glass window, so I couldn't see hardly anything other than that the lights were on in the kitchen, and I thought I might've heard music and maybe even voices, so I started pounding on the door, all the while calling for Larry. I kept yellin' and poundin' yellin' and pounding, for the longest time.

Clara

The water from the sink felt cool, which was a blessing. I looked down at the pool on the floor, thinking, "It's going to take me forever to clean this mess up." "Funny what goes through your mind at times like this," I thought. As I continued to look down, I noticed bits of black stuff collecting in the water at my feet. I wondered if I was seeing pieces of my burnt clothes, or patches of my burnt skin. The smoke seemed to be getting thicker by the minute. I tried to ask the boy if he'd shut the front door, but it was obvious to me, even in my confused state, that he'd left it wide open, allowing the fire and smoke to follow us in. Somewhere in the back of my mind I could hear pounding, and somebody was calling a name, but I couldn't make it out. Looking at the water, I suddenly imagined myself in a boat slowly drifting away from shore. I looked over at the boy. I could barely see him for the smoke, even though I knew he was still standing close by. He seemed to be looking down now, too. His arms were hanging loose at his sides, and his sprayer was aimed at the floor.

Tommy

There was no sign of Robert comin' back yet, and not one car had passed. I had to do something, so I ran down the back steps, across the yard, and into the garden. I was looking for somthin' I could use to smash the back door's window. I couldn't find but little stones, which wouldn't have done it, but there were some fair-size pumpkins, so I grabbed one of those, broke its stalk, and carried it to the back door. "Boy, am I gonna be in trouble for this," I thought. I threw the pumpkin at the window as hard as I could, and ducked away from any glass splinters. It went right through, and the music got suddenly louder. "Great!" I thought, "Now I can help, too." My plan was to carefully reach through the broken window and open the door from the inside, but I never got that far. As soon as the glass broke, I heard this whooshing noise come from inside. That's the only way I could describe it—a loud "whoosh!" Right then, the whole kitchen lit up with fire and a big cloud of black smoke came pouring out. I backed up and fell on the grass, choking and spluttering. I got back up and got as close as I could, but the whole place seemed to be on fire now. I kept calling "Larry" as loud as I could, but there wasn't any answer. I went back out front to where I left my bike and sat on the grass. There wasn't anything else I could do. The music had stopped by then.

Clara

The last thing I remember was a strong gust of wind that threw me and the boy against each other. I wrapped my arms around him and drew him into my boat. He looked up at me and mouthed the words, "I'm sorry." And then the two of us drifted away.

Lester

Larry and Clara talk often. Tommy and Robert sometimes visit both.

Peter Welch

Boyhood, Belonging, Becoming

In this tender coming of age memoir, Peter Welch immerses the reader in mid-20th century Maine, a world of Saturday morning cartoons and records that play on turnstiles, instant coffee and cigarettes, and long afternoons outdoors with siblings and neighbors. Welch deftly reconstructs this past, limiting much of the reader's experience to his own pre-adolescent sense-making. With Welch, we observe the ritual performances of masculinity. We feel the pressure to adhere to the unspoken rules enforced in the bus, bathroom, and gymnasium—rules Welch doesn't fully understand, but that other boys and men know implicitly. Skillfully layered across these snapshots is the author's budding sexuality, the growing realization that he is gay, the sense that he is "a different kind of boy." Balancing the delights of childhood and the crushing pressures to conform, Welch celebrates the agency and growth that accompanies risk-taking as he finds his way to his own unique becoming. MAC

I spy Mrs. Boston, my first-grade teacher, as she tacitly moves around the room, inspecting hands for clipped and clean fingernails. She lands at my desk and, like the other students, I offer her my hands, though my fingers are curled under. She slides her own nimble hand under my two and gently fans out mine, revealing chipped remnants of shiny pink nail polish at the end of my long fingers. I can only look down. In the bathroom prior to this surprise inspection, I scratched and scraped as much off as I was able, but it's still there.

In a faint voice she asks, "What's this?" I don't answer and keep looking down at my fingers, ready for this moment to be over. From the corner of my eye, I watch her body straighten, still holding my hands in her own, considering me. She's tilted her head; her face has a curious expression. Eventually, I look up, making brief eye contact before she moves on to the next student.

Then as now, I have no memory of painting my fingernails with pink polish when I am six. Perhaps I have discovered glossy nail paint in my sister's or mother's room and experimented with it on my own fingernails. I am a boy and understand that boys don't wear nail polish. Still, my fingernails are painted pink! Am I now marked by the teacher and the other students sitting nearby who have witnessed this exchange? Fortunately, no teasing occurs. Mrs. Boston remains kind to me after this discovery. I imagine it is alright that a boy in her first-grade class has painted his fingernails with a bit of shiny pink nail polish. Maybe it will be okay to be a different kind of boy here.

❖　❖　❖

While mum is driving, she peers into the rearview mirror and casually offers, "Don't kiss your grandfather on the lips." My mother and brother and I are traveling to Sanford, Maine, a short ride from where we live in Moody, to visit our grandfather Roberge. We go to see her father every few months, an obligatory visit in an attempt to maintain a relationship with him, and perhaps have him come to know his grandsons.

As she makes this remark, I'm sitting on the edge of the back seat, and our eyes briefly meet in the mirror. I feel my face flush, a mixture of shame and confusion. I only know that what she has said is weird, causing me to sit back next to my brother and ponder my confused thoughts. Paul seems to be in his own world, looking out the window. I imagine he's heard Mum's comment but keeps to himself.

Have I kissed Grampa on the lips before?

Don't family members sometimes kiss each other?

Is she saying this to teach me that boys aren't supposed to kiss other boys on the lips, and if we do, will it be terrible for everyone?

◆ ◆ ◆

I dash toward the swing set with my brother and our friends Ruthie and Cathy. This is our morning ritual. The cobalt September sky is clear, the day sunny, but cool. Still, I tear off my jacket and run along the set of swings to find a place among my friends.

At my swing, I push myself off, dust mixing with excitement as I pump my legs, stretching them out in front toward the open sky. My legs are lean and strong and will carry me anywhere, to the blue air and back again. I hold the swing chains tightly, leaning back while flying forward and up, my body lifting from the seat, defying gravity. In an instant, at the crest of my swing, I tuck my legs under and begin the descent, to center and up again, this time in reverse, as the swing's arc completes itself. The wind whooshes past my ears. I look to both sides and catch the half-moon of motion my brother and friends create as their own arcs glide through the air. We swing and whirl, our movements separate but together, a dance of gravity and momentum, and friendship. When we simultaneously reach the crest, we squeal with delight. We are free.

All too soon, the bell rings and recess is over. I slow the pumping of my legs and decide to jump at the top of my swing arc. I'm anxious with excitement. In an instant, I release the chains from my hands, flying through time and space, the air whizzing past as I land with a thud on the playground's sandy surface. Dust explodes around me. I wipe my hands off, grab my jacket, and head inside with Paul, Ruthie, and Cathy for our next lesson.

The sense of freedom those few minutes provide lingers through the day, blooming into a smile I can't contain; pure joy rising up from my body.

* * *

Perched at the sliding glass door, I peek out from inside the house, onto the driveway where my father convenes with other men from the neighborhood, along with their sons. They are eyeballing his new motorcycle.

The air is cold and biting. The boys and men hover close together. Plumes of breath rise, a dispersing cloud of vapor mingling above their huddled bodies. Even from the house, I see my dad's swelling chest, his murmuring of "CC's . . . torque . . . new skins." He kicks up the kick stand with ease and mounts the Kawi, both feet firmly planted on the ground to hold up its mass. His hands travel across the bike, inspecting the hog's instrument panel and fuel tank to make sure there's enough gas for a long, low ride. He talks jovially with his pals as they nudge each other, enamored with this new man-toy.

I am a boy of ten, and like other boys my age, am wondering where I fit into the life of my father. I'd like to understand how he might love me, and I him.

Though I already know this is not my tribe.

Dad rides the kickstart, lifting his entire body, and thrusts, spurring the engine as it smoothly turns over. He gives the throttle a few deep turns as the mufflers echo throughout the neighborhood. The bike's exhaust adds foggy plume to the chilly air, mixing with the collective breath of boys and men. Excitement among them is brimming over as they circle my dad and tousle each other. Perhaps they are wondering who will get the first ride.

Later into adulthood, I will come to understand that my father is often unsure of himself among his 'best buddies.' The unease he carries of his own identity and place in the world, his sense of genuine belonging, will barely make its way to the surface during his lifetime.

I peer from behind the glass as this spirited exchange plays itself out. I briefly consider joining them, then rethink the idea, lingering from a safe distance. I've seen this ritual before, dozens of times, and understand that it is a requirement of fitting in, one of the many rites of passage for boys and men not like me.

I watch my dad struggle to navigate the space between me and him, and him and his buddies. Perhaps my softness reminds him of his own tender underbelly. Like the rest of us, he's learned the ugly epithets—*fag* mostly, and how he and his buddies talk about and treat women, like objects. A calendar of scantily clothed women in provocative poses hangs in the basement next to his workbench. It reminds me of something you might find behind the counter in a greasy auto mechanic shop.

To his credit, Dad does his best to keep these aspects of himself separate from his boys. He never encourages us to ogle the women in the calendar, thank goodness. Still, his guise of masculinity creates miles between us, an emotional cavern that interferes with meaningful connection between father and son. I understand this hidden side of him because I, too, am learning to navigate the stifling culture of manhood with its rigid rules and rituals.

I take one last look outside, then turn away.

❖　❖　❖

"Get bent!" barks Virginia.

I ride in the bus seat in front of her and her friend Lynn on our way home from school one day. I have turned around to gaze at them, curious about their girl-conversation, their physical closeness in the seat as they huddle in gossip and friendship. Boys don't huddle like this, unless it's on the playing field, their focus a football, basketball, or baseball. My requisite smile does little to assuage their collective contempt for me in this moment. What is wrong with being curious about their friendship? It seems that, for now at least, girls only have friendships with other girls. Boys too. For me, friendships with other boys is messy and difficult. I don't know why. I don't understand what *Get Bent* means, though Virginia says it like "Fuck you, you little faggot!" I turn around, bending back, humiliated and confused.

◆ ◆ ◆

We boys snake through the entrance of Moody Store single file, searching for our dads. Louie, from behind the counter, without looking up from perusing the *York County Coast Star*, points to the back. Ricky races ahead, followed by the rest of us, and he's the first to arrive at the wide floor-to-ceiling door with its heavy metal latch. The walk-in fridge. He lifts the latch and we make our way in. Along with Bimmy, the story owner, our dads are there, standing in a semicircle, facing the entrance, each nursing a Bud Light.

One by one, we take our places in the tidy frigid space, alongside crates of milk, eggs, cartons of wine, and stacks and stacks of beer. Our presence expands the arc, now becoming a circle of boys and men standing close. I quash the urge to shiver.

My father holds his beer can close against his belly. We make brief eye contact, but that is all. He seems embarrassed that I have discovered this curious hive where he and his cronies gather, talking about whatever men do while they tend to their beers so early in the day. For a few minutes, we stand around and gawk, making small talk. Eventually, our boy ringleader Ricky casually asks, "when do you know you're a man," and one of the other boys blurts out, "pubic hair," and everybody chuckles. Then, Ricky, his head held high, proclaims, "Well, I'm a man then!" Another round of laughter. And with that, we boys take our leave from the walk-in, marching out as if we've been dismissed from duty. I'm relieved. It was chilly in there, and kind of boring.

Dad and I never talk about this encounter. I wonder if he thought about it at all. I wonder if he considered coming home that day and sitting down with my brother and me and asking us if we had any questions about our lives as boys who are becoming men. Maybe he would have shared his own challenges, the hurdles he encountered in becoming a man himself. Maybe he would have invited us to ask him anything, anything at all. And if he could help to ease the transition, he would certainly do whatever he could to make life easier for us, as boys on the verge of manhood.

◆   ◆   ◆

Our Zenith color TV sits against the basement family room's east wall. A revered piece of furniture in its own right, the 21" sage-green screen is bookended between tall, rectangular speakers whose interior oval outline you can make out, in the right light, through the tight cloth mesh that covers them. The entertainment center, enshrined in polished oak, is steadied on four spindly oak legs with shiny brass feet. The couch, and side accent chairs, and black vinyl beanbag chair we siblings covet, all face the TV. Zenith is an altar of sorts, paying homage to the almighty picture box and the stories projected for our consumption until we are stuffed and full. The TV's pinnacle is an aqua blue lava lamp.

There are television shows, quotidian favorites, that my brother, sister, and I religiously watch as we rush home from school—*Dark Shadows*, *Gilligan's Island*, *The Brady Bunch*, in that order, all before supper. We are free from worry about Dad's drinking, or wondering if Mum will be too tired to hear about my day when she arrives home from work. Through the TV's relentless tug, we follow the yellow-brick road to an enchanted land or imagine ourselves inhabiting a deserted island. The stories from the talking box are adventures we collectively share.

While we are at school, our grandmother spies her own darlings—*Days of our Lives* is her favorite. She's reluctant to admit being hooked on these soapy storylines, but on days when I am home from school, we watch together.

TV after supper is reserved for our parents, who begin with the evening news, then a game show followed by a movie-of-the-week. We kids sometimes join them. Every year, we patiently wait for *The Wizard of Oz* to air its national broadcast, on a Sunday night early in the year, with no commercial interruptions. We put a temporary hold on whatever else that occupies us and huddle together for this viewing event.

On the weekends, Saturday morning cartoons hold the rapt attention of me and my siblings. We follow the shenanigans of Bugs Bunny or the Road Runner, the futuristic possibilities of The Jetsons, and the slapstick adventures of Scooby-Doo. We are rambunctious in our laughter and joy of being together. We wrestle over who owns the beanbag chair, and if we can't agree, sit close and split the beans down the middle.

We are reminded when we plant ourselves on top of the TV that it will ruin our eyes if we don't back away. We care little for this adult insight and wedge ourselves as close as we possibly can, mesmerized by its psychic and spectra-color pull. On Sundays, the TV is commandeered by my dad, who believes he enjoys watching football. Within a few minutes of the start of a game, he's fast asleep, stretched out on the couch, snoring away.

My siblings and I carefully follow every word of a blended family as they manage their own weekly crisis and eventually come to a thoughtful resolution in less than thirty minutes, including an important moral lesson. Though I understand that *The Brady Bunch* is fictional entertainment, I appreciate the myriad ways that they, as a family, manage challenging situations with aplomb.

During Season Three, Peter Brady's voice begins to change. "Dough Re Mi" is the episode's title. Every time Peter attempts to sing the song his brother Greg has written, the middle Brady's voice cracks at "Mi." I am eleven, a year or so shy of my own voice's transformation and am absorbed in the episode's unfolding. Plus, Peter and I share a name. Eventually, Peter and his five siblings decide to spotlight his changing voice in the song's recording of "The Brady Six." The episode's message resonates with me: as a family, your special qualities are celebrated. Sour lemons become delicious lemonade. I long for this kind of love and appreciation in my own family.

*   *   *

Wayne hammers on my friend Gerald. His assault is not physical but psychological and emotional. At the desk behind him, Wayne snarls "faggot" over and over in a low murmur as to go unnoticed by the teacher Mrs. Hunt. He pokes Gerald in the shoulder with his pencil eraser at each utterance of the ugly epithet. Gerald does his best to shrug him off, then finally turns around and squeals, "Leave me alone."

The rest of the class is working on a writing assignment, bone-silent before this declaration. The teacher only shushes Gerald, then offers a grumpy reminder for all of us to get back to work. I'm sitting at the desk in the row next to Gerald. From the corner of my eye, I've witnessed this transaction and have done nothing to help. Wayne scares me too, so I keep my mouth shut through my dear friend's misery. I'm a coward, and not ready to confront anyone, never mind a bully like Wayne. What if he thinks I'm a fag? Then what?

At recess later that day, Gerald and I race for the tall swings and claim our spot among other swingers. We are each ready to expel some energy. The swings welcome us as we pump our legs as fast as we're able. Who will be the first to reach the blue sky above us? We laugh and scream into the air, relinquishing our worry into the afternoon atmosphere.

*   *   *

Mum and Dad are talking, their voices muffled and low in the kitchen above us. There's an occasional ratchet of volume by one or the other. It's difficult to understand their words, but I know they are arguing. Curiosity and concern carry me up the cellar stairs two at a time. At the top, I enter the kitchen and assess the situation. Dad is hunched at the sliding glass door, looking out toward the street, contemplating some momentary or permanent burden. It's hard to tell. The outline of his rough hands stretched against his blue-jean pockets. His checkered gray flannel shirt is disheveled. A cigarette hangs from his lips, his face is scruffy and unshaven. A haze of smoke swirls around him, and I crinkle my nose in a silent protest of his two-pack-a-day habit.

Behind us, my mother urges herself around the kitchen, preparing her own breakfast—instant coffee and a slice of toast she slathers with butter that will melt just enough. Mum is cocooned in a mint green quilted bathrobe, wrapped head-to-toe in polyester-blend. Her brown bouffant hair is matted in the back from a night of mangled sleep. Her eyes are fixed across the room, peering at my dad while perched at the counter sipping her black coffee, poker-faced. A hush now envelops the room. The air is warm and taut, like an overinflated balloon ready to explode at the slightest provocation.

I look to my father, breaking the silence to say, "Hey Dad, wanna go outside and play awhile?" He takes a long puff, then pulls the cigarette from his mouth, turns his head toward me, says nothing. His gaze moves back to the world outside. Gravity pulls tobacco ash to the floor while smoke wafts around him, lingering.

What is he looking at I wonder? I wait for his answer, watching him as I lean against the glass door's cold metal frame, arms crossed, heart thumping. Smoke curls between us. I linger, my breathing frozen. A few seconds pass, though it feels longer. From across the room, in between crunchy bites of buttery toast and long sips of cooling black coffee, Mum barks at me, "Leave him alone." I instantly believe that the room's psychic density has something to do with me, some behavior or action I did or didn't do to cause them to act in this strange and confusing way. My wish to play outside with my dad has been warped into something menacing, a seismic weight hovering in this odd moment.

"What do you think, Dad?" I look up to him, a last-ditch effort at connection and possibility. A minute passes. I want to beat him with my fists, crying out with every ounce of my being, to see the boy who only wants his father's attention. Simultaneously, I wish to disappear from the kitchen, pretending this exchange never occurred. *Never mind,* I think to myself. I catapult myself down the stairs, two at a time, to the basement where I'll watch Saturday morning cartoons in the good company of my brother and sister. I am deflated by the exchange with my parents but sidestep my disappointment and become absorbed in the crazy antics of Road Runner and Wile E. Coyote.

◆　◆　◆

Before boys morph into men, sometime during adolescence when they become skittish in friendships with boys like my brother and me, soft boys, kind boys, Paul and I enjoy sleepovers with our neighbor and friend Peter G. We hang out with him and his younger sister Janie, either at our house or theirs, watching *Gilligan's Island, I Dream of Jeannie,* and *Star Trek.* We play hide-and-seek, tag, or Monopoly. We create inside forts out of backward-facing chairs covered in old blankets, and outside structures among the grove of pine trees between our neighboring houses.

I am obsessed with Karen Carpenter and her brother Richard, the singing siblings The Carpenters. Karen's voice is sultry, and Richard's dimples and backup vocals accompany his sister in a perfect musical duo. Their song lyrics gush with emotions that confirm my burgeoning identity as a boy who likes other boys. It seems as if Karen and Richard are singing to me about life's complex and winding roads. On Dick Clark's *American Bandstand,* I watch transfixed as Karen sings and plays the drums. She's got it all.

One Saturday night, Paul and I lug our sleeping bags next door to Peter G's house for an overnight. We sleep in the basement, a room with floor tiles and unfinished white walls. It's far enough away from the rest of his family upstairs to feel as if we are on an adventure. The physical space is incomplete, like us as boys who are not yet men. As we settle in, I arrange the sleeping cots around the record player, and put on the 45 record, "We've Only Just Begun." After a dozen times listening to "a kiss for luck and we're on our way…" I flip the record to the backside, "Hurting Each Other," another aching ballad that wraps itself around me.

Paul and Peter groan at the music's repetition but are patient with me, somehow understanding the importance of my playing that record over and over, way past midnight.

I later learn that the song "We've Only Just Begun" is the story of a newly married couple, hope expressed for the beginning of their lives, working day-to-day, together. I feel so much potential in listening to the lyrics, not necessarily in finding a perfect partner and living a happily-ever-after life, but in the sense that my own life is just beginning. What I can only describe as a trust in myself starts to take hold. I am beginning to believe I will one day understand what togetherness means, my place in the scheme of things. My own belonging.

❖   ❖   ❖

He leans against the gray bathroom wall, the space sculpted from days of holding court, his shadow forever inked here. If he stands long enough, he will surely meld into an outline of himself, permanently etched into the concrete blocks of the boy's bathroom. With one leg firmly planted on the pale green floor, the other bent, his foot against the wall, he's flanked by his ruffian cronies. His arms are crossed over his chest, appearing relaxed among his boy pals. A smirk blooms from his pockmarked puss as I walk by.

I bring my best poker-face to these unsettling seconds, briefly making eye contact. My heart is already in my throat. I move past him and his buddies with casual intention as I trek toward the urinals to take care of business. I consider using one of the two adjacent stalls, though neither has a working door, so think better of it.

I step up to the urinal next to the metal panel that separates them from the toilets. A minor refuge. Speckles of rust colonize the divider where urine has splashed, paint corroded from years of boys with questionable aim. I unzip my pants, pull out my penis and wait. My heart thumps. Pulses of fear rise up from a churning belly and becomes bile in the back of my throat. I swallow hard. Pearls of sweat threaten to bead on my forehead and upper lip.

The space is dingy, weathered paint chipping everywhere. I inspect the tattered gray wall an inch from my nose. I discover places where paint has dripped and dried. The graffiti, variations of *fag*, and *suck my dick*, have been scribbled and partially scrubbed away. I visualize my next class, math with Mrs. Ridder. I gaze up at the stained white ceiling. A silent prayer. Nothing. Dead silence drones the bathroom. I imagine this line of boys behind me, snickering. A musky-yellow light slices in from the high translucent windows, a looming spotlight on the three urinals against the wall. Lysol, septic, and bravado crowd the room, making it difficult to breathe.

Then, from his perch against the bathroom wall, the grand master declares, "Having difficulties?" He stretches the word *difficulties*, adding syllables. I hear a 'Grinch smile' on his face as his words linger and infect the air. He is basking in this small, precious victory. After a few, piercing seconds, his boy cronies break into collective laughter, hyenas in a gang howl. Their cackles echo through my head as I push hard on the flush, tuck myself back into my pants, zip up, and carry my humiliation with me out the door. I make my way to math class where I will become fluent in adding, subtracting, multiplying, and dividing whole numbers, fractions, and decimals, understanding the relationships between them. Midway through the lesson, I ask Mrs. Ridder if I can use the bathroom. I'll have a better chance of some privacy there during class.

◆　◆　◆

I am gangly, without much meat on my frame. In fact, one of my friends, Julie G., routinely offers a playful punch to my skinny arm, calling me a "bag of bones." My shoe size surges weekly. There are new pimples on my face each morning when I look in the mirror. Adolescence has arrived. One day perusing a magazine, I discover an exercise device advertised in the back pages. Alongside the ad is a picture of a fit, muscular man, wearing only a pair of dark, tight shorts. He reminds me of Tarzan from the movies I watch on the weekends. The ad's copy reads, "You, too, can look like Mr. Atlas!! Order today." I briefly consider my body, then complete the order form, enclose a $20 bill, and mail off for my future physique and new life as the boy who can do anything in Phys. Ed. class. Along with the other strong boys, I will one day mount the dastardly climbing rope that dangles from the gymnasium ceiling.

Within a week or so, my destiny arrives in the mail. I open the package feeling excited and hopeful, ready to develop my new, muscular body. On one end of the device, a long, thick rope is threaded through a plastic hand grip. The firmer the user's grip, the more difficult it becomes to pull the rope. The device requires that I work against my own resistance. The other end of the rope holds two nylon loops, made to secure your feet in place while you pull.

I am self-conscious about my intentions to build my body. I decide to utilize the device in our basement closet, away from the gaze of any curious family members, even my brother. Over the next few months, I embark on a "squeeze and pull" routine to add girth to my tall frame. I dedicate an hour each day and perform individual exercises designed to make me bigger. I wait for the transformative effects of my daily efforts of squeezing and pulling the rope. Any changes that occur with my body from here-on-out are within my hands and the tension I create in them. The harder I squeeze, the more muscle I will gain.

After a few weeks, or maybe longer, I become bored with the squeezing and pulling and am noticing little change in my body. I come to the conclusion that the device is a hoax.

Still, working out is my "pass" into the lives of other boys and men. Because I am tall, it's expected that I will play basketball, though my hand-eye coordination is terrible. I'm in awe of other boys who are able to bounce the basketball (without watching it) while they simultaneously run across the court from one hoop to the other. During basketball tryouts, a few of the older boys hurl the ball at me and my brother, a test to see if we can keep up. The basketball ricochets off our hands, confirmation to them that we aren't part of the pack. A simple test of boyhood that we fail. Later, a new Phys. Ed. teacher, Mr. Hankel, initiates a winter track program which I enthusiastically join. Here, I excel as an athlete in individual events that enrich both me and the team.

◆ ◆ ◆

A stand of white pines separates our house from the neighbor's. My brother and I meet Peter and Janie among the trees where we create our own kid's community in this shared neck of the woods. Today, we score scrap pine boards to build a tree fort. To begin the project, we identify a cluster of four trees with enough girth to hold a structure off the ground, something we'll climb up into.

After our measuring and hammering, then making final adjustments to be sure the fort will hold our weight, we tack an old blanket scrap over the entrance and shimmy our way up and inside. The space is darker than I imagined. Still, the day's light finds points of entry along edges and knots in the wood. I scurry into the house to grab pillows so the fort feels cozier, a home away from home.

On other days, in this shared cluster of trees between our homes, we create imaginary rooms on the forest floor. During these projects, we draw out our imagined space with the edge of a tree branch, used like a pencil in the dirt. Dropped pine needles augment the demarcations, as we pile them to create the idea of rooms—a cottage with a living room, bedroom, and kitchen. We collect rocks and construct a stone walkway or fire pit. Weathered pine cones are everywhere, so we gather them into a stone circle, imagining a fire there. A bundle of pine needles raked with our fingers acts as a bed or sofa, a soft place to lie back and gaze at the tree canopy above, moving in the wind, sunlight dappling across our young bodies.

A few weeks later, our cousin David visits with his mom, our favorite aunt, Anita. She is statuesque and fun-loving and owns her own beauty shop in the basement of her home in Colchester, Connecticut. She teaches us about independent women by living her life on her own terms. Her son David is feral and shares his wildness with us when they travel north to Maine for a visit.

On a breezy afternoon, David and Paul and I squeeze into the newly constructed tree fort, relaxing and playing it cool in the confines of our tiny house among the white pines. David reaches into his pants pocket and with a wry smile, pulls out a few Kools, menthol cigarettes he pinched from his mother's purse when she wasn't looking. He strikes a match and lights his own cigarette with confidence and ease, then passes me and my brother each one, along with a matchbook. I tear a match from the inside cover, swipe it along the front striker, and hurriedly bring the cigarette to my mouth. I draw on the filter with all my might, hoping to ignite the tobacco on the first match. "Suck on it! Suck on it!," David urges as he pulls his own cigarette from his mouth, a manly clench between his thumb and index finger. With the second match, I spy an orange glow at the end of my cigarette.

My first inhalation brings a sputter and cough as my lungs recalibrate, stinging from the tar and nicotine I've ingested. "Pussy," David casually offers. Now, I'm determined to keep this cigarette lit! The taste of mint and tobacco is a weird combination, and I puff and puff. After a few drags, a sucking-in which causes a glint of the cigarette's ember, I lift my head, then exhale. I'm a cool cat now. The smoke casually lifts through the dim light of the fort's interior, drawn to the crevices and knot holes, pulled like a vacuum into the atmosphere where it dissipates into nothingness.

✦ ✦ ✦

In the locker room, we boys have finished changing into our T-shirts, shorts, and sneakers, waiting for Mr. Foley to tell us what we'll be doing today in gym class. I'm betting on dodge ball. A cluster of boy bodies has gathered around David J., a popular boy among us. He is physically mature for his age, with hair under his arms and a patch at his groin. His body leans toward muscular. We all want to *be* David J. and will say or do anything he asks.

For a laugh, David demonstrates the manly way to inspect one's fingernails for trimming. But before he shares this great insight, he directs us to check our own fingernails. If we do it the right way, we're real boys becoming men. The wrong way means we are fags. I am unsure of the correct answer, so wait and watch, holding my breath. Other boys demonstrate: palm towards yourself, fingers curled inward. The beginning of a fist.

Boys police other boys' behavior with nagging persistence and regularity. It's difficult to know when something I do will be interrogated by another boy as not being boy-ly enough. I watch myself with great vigilance while in the company of other boys.

◆ ◆ ◆

My heart is racing as I wake from a dream at around 1 a.m. My mind is foggy. My breath caught in my throat. The dream ricochets through my brain, bare chests and boys clustered among each other. I'm rattled. Paul is asleep in the bed next to me, lightly snoring. The air in our bedroom is warm and close. My next movements are cautious and slow. I gently pull back the covers and get out of bed. I change into a T-shirt and shorts, bring my sneakers to my chest and tiptoe out of our room, down the hallway, and through the living room and kitchen. Then, I pull the sliding glass door open, just enough to squeeze through. I make my way outside where I put on and lace up my sneakers. The three-quarter moon is opaque behind night clouds, enough light to see directly in front of me as my eyes adjust to the night.

There are rumors from contemptuous local boys that men gather in the Ogunquit beach dunes at night. I walk the mile or so east from my house to the beach, then travel another mile or so south until I reach the dunes where men gather. I feel dazed and have been observing myself since I woke up and ventured into an abyss. I am alone in the middle of the night, exploring the unknown around and within me. I am inside my body and also outside of it. The voice in my head wonders what I'm looking for, what I'll discover once I reach the dunes where men gather. The air is balmy, and the light breeze off the Atlantic cools my body and carries me through the soft, fine sand along the water's edge. What I am doing feels both dangerous and exciting. Despite the August heat, my teeth chatter.

I arrive at the spot in the dunes where I suspect that men gather and make my way up the sandy hillside into the belly of the night. Through an ink-blue haze, body silhouettes begin to appear among the irregular sand-dune formations. They dart back and forth as if playing a game of hide and seek. In the near distance, patches of tall dune grass conceal bodies crouched low, motionless and watching, their senses honed, like mine, each of us unsure of the other's next move. The bodies observe and wait. I stand still, quietly inspecting my surroundings. I have come across some new knowledge or experience that I don't quite understand. I'm a curious tourist who has inadvertently discovered a strange and provocative new human species, capable of possibilities beyond my teenage imagination. I breathe through my skin, slow and steady, like a fawn who suddenly meets a stranger in the woods. Fear billows throughout my body.

Then, simply, I turn around and make my way back down the dune hill to the beach below. The moon has expressed herself through the clouds, gently pulling me in a new direction. I am aware of ocean waves breaking, an intermittent and forever whoosh. A dome of stars becomes my guide as I walk north along the ocean's edge. Then I travel a mile or so west back to my house. I open the sliding glass door, enough to squeeze through, and move silently through the kitchen and living room, down the hallway, and into the bedroom I share with my brother. I climb back into bed and eventually fall asleep.

❖ ❖ ❖

It's just after lunch on a warm, early-summer day in June. Billowy clouds inch across a cerulean sky. School is out and my brother Paul and I amble through our backyard, looking for mischief. We have come to love climbing trees. It's a way to exert ourselves outdoors in the natural world and compete to see who can climb the highest. We are tall and skinny, not unlike these towering wonders of roots and trunks and branches. The adults tell us we grow like weeds.

Our tree climbing offers freedom, too, from any turmoil inside the house, Mum and Dad arguing, or worse, the silent treatment between them. We gain a new perspective up there, going out on the limbs of the tree and also onto the precipice of our boyhood as we test the possibilities—will this branch hold me? Will anyone know that we are here among the clouds? Being high in the trees is also a place where we can spy on the actions of our family without being noticed.

A grove of Eastern White Pine trees is perched on a small hill behind our house, inviting us over for a closer inspection. At their base, I gaze up through a gnarl of branches where a spattering of sky reaches in along the trees' vertical pull. The wind stirs their reaching upper limbs. This stand of trees stretches forty, fifty feet into the atmosphere and their girth resembles a mingling of sturdy adult men. The pines have rugged trunks and capable horizontal branches. We've climbed these wondrous trees before, but never to the top.

"Hey, Paul, are you ready to climb?" I ask.

"Ready," he enthusiastically replies, peering up into the belly of the tree.

Today we decide we're going all the way up.

"Can you give me a hand?"

Paul provides a hoist to the first branch and it manages to hold my boy weight, then I offer him a hand up. With some wrangling, we each make it to the next row of bulky branches. Dark patches of pine pitch already cover our fingers and palms. I've scraped my forearm on the course tree bark and my skin there is ruffed up, but so far, no blood. My brother and I move with steady intention, grunting and breathing heavily with each careful maneuver.

We reach and pull to the next level of branches and soon find ourselves in the protective interior of this massive conifer. The horizontal limbs easily hold our weight. We are acrobats maneuvering up and through tangled tree topography. I'm aware of the importance of holding on, and what could happen if I suddenly let go or misstep one branch to the next. About midway to the tree's crown, I twist around and peer through the branch arms, out across the yard.

"Wow!" is all we say to each other, our eyes wide at each other, our mouths a silent "O" as we look up and out. The aerial view feels magnificent.

I see the rooftop of our house, the swaying branches of neighboring trees down the yard, and just beyond, the grassy field across the street. I find the stone wall that runs along our house's road frontage, then further out, a scattering of rooftops leading to Route One, the major roadway through town. The new perspective energizes me, and I turn back around to focus on the task at hand: climbing to the top.

As we continue up, the branches become thinner—wiry, like us. We move through scraggly limbs, aware that there's less tree and more air and sky surrounding us. With one hand, I hold tightly to what looks to be a strong branch, and with the other, wrap my arm around the tree's shrinking girth. I scrape my other arm on the rough, knotty bark. No harm done. My feet are firmly planted on two separate limbs, albeit at different heights. Blotches of dark pine pitch cover my hands. I smell my fingers and breathe in the tree's turpentine scent—pungent, acidic, and sweet. I am feeling both exhilarated and terrified, higher into the tree canopy than ever before. Holding tight, I turn my upper body to look out into the distance, past a cluster of houses to a sea foam marsh where water undulates, riverlike, a row of beach cottages, smaller still, along the Atlantic's edge. Then, only ocean vastness, reaching to the horizon.

We climb down the tree in a matter of minutes. Why is the descent easier to navigate?

I am satisfied with my new accomplishment—climbing all the way to the top. I'm satisfied to have reached past my fear of falling. Satisfied to have maneuvered this great pine, my courage growing with each gnarly branch I climb. Satisfied to now see my street, and neighborhood and town in this new light that makes it all feel bigger somehow. Satisfied that while climbing, I realize I am becoming a part of the tree, becoming another branch or limb, leaning and connected where limbs meet trunk, communing.

Abbie Kiefer

Better Homes, Better Gardens

As a daughter whose mother has died and as a mother with her own young children, the speaker in Abbie Kiefer's poems positions the traditional Yankee pragmatism in which she was raised against the pop-culture purveyors of domestic perfection—the Martha Stewarts who dictate, for example, "the only right way to fold a fitted sheet" and "the correct level of dampness for a compost pile." (Regarding the former, Kiefer writes with winking irony, "Making / a bed, I pull the sheets taut as a smile.") These poems address her desire for permanence in a world where the possibility of loss is ever-present and there is "no easy possession of truth." Out of the precise details of her home's "proximate clutter" and her garden's unsparing seasonal bounty, Kiefer crafts lines of lean, Shaker-like elegance. "Yield is its own antonym: what I produce, what I surrender," she proclaims. I am grateful for the gift of this poet's steely wisdom and generous heart. RF

My Hundred-Year Flood

On a bridge newly risen
from the current's rough cover,
we watched the river. Its continuing

urgency. I was just beginning
to feel bored when the Kennebec bore forward
a fridge—that strange craft cutting,

I know now,
toward Merrymeeting Bay. Then on
to the Atlantic, which must take so often

into its cold plenty
something like this—a person's particular
and once-essential belonging. My parents offered

a name: hundred-year flood.
Not again while we're alive they said
but at seven, *lifetime* flared itself

wide like the river carrying
a fridge carrying apples and a jar of mustard
and a wrapped square of cake,

small holes in the frosting
where the candles had been. I didn't think
of it then—the food, or the forty miles

to Phippsburg, where the river's mouth
always delivers its truth.
I didn't know it would return

to me, that slow-sinking Whirlpool,
in my sometimes-
spells of indeterminate sadness.

A metal box in the chop—
it's how I started to learn
uncertainty. My mother holding my hand

as it went under my feet.

On *The Early Show,* Martha Stewart Explains How to Keep a Home

When she demonstrates the only right way to fold a fitted sheet, I covet her confidence. The easy possession of truth. She pockets one corner in another, smooths the strata conclusively. I'm teaching my boys to fold clothes, Minecraft t-shirts and knee-thinned jeans—each attempt a wrinkled mess, as my mom would have said. She ironed most of what she wore. Liked how cotton so gladly unfurrowed under warmth. Liked talking with me while she passed the slick plate over fabric, her finished work stacked into appreciable piles. She'd offer me the board; I said the piles were just made to diminish. To be diminished, wear by wear. I wasn't wrong but oh, I was smug. Martha insists on a daily-made bed. Believes a taut coverlet and primmed pillows discourage proximate clutter—balled socks, scattered papers. My papers: always scattered. Loose lines on torn slips and leafed piles I want, wildly, to make appreciable. German-crafted journals fanned open like hands, every finger a middle one. This is the work that calls me. It's a clamor and demanding as my boys believe me to be when I demonstrate how one pant leg should square with the other, when I say this work has value, and are any of us convinced? *Your turn* I tell them, itching to take over. To dispense with the task myself, in silence. The trouble with a fitted sheet, its elasticized hem: it will always want to draw toward itself. Though Martha insists it can be conquered, pulling the parcel to her chest. The audience claps.

On *House Hunters,* the Buyers Always Insist They'll Need Space for Entertaining

We hunted houses
    for cracks. Cellars for damp. Figured the age of roofs
and how long
    they might hold. *Can you picture your lives here* the agent asked
and did we nod? Standing
    in the center of empty spaces. Pretending to render
our eventual selves.
    Our house's first owner: the agent's ex. She never knew him
to be reasonable
    but he took what we offered. Sold us seven rooms on two
floors on two
    wooded acres—the spaces where we like to entertain
ourselves:
    click Legos, grow lettuce. Deal the cards, fan them full.
For birthdays
    I serve lemon cake, uncandled—no bright thing
needlessly extinguished.
    Last day of December, we kiss well before midnight.
Let the new year bring itself in.

The Possibility of Loss

When he was four,
our boy became embarrassed
by sadness. *Ha!* he'd bark,
tearing up. *Ha ha!*
Like when he told us
that he'd never leave home
because all his Legos are here,
his voice lurching on *Legos*,
body blurring upstairs
when I moved
to hold him. *So funny,* you said.
Yes, I barked. *Ha ha.*

A Brief History of Yankee Thrift, Yankee Ingenuity, and Yankee Work Ethic

To make. To make do or do without. To trust your own two hands, maybe too much. To save the bent nails in coffee cans. To fold the ratty towels. To value the threadbaring towels and the labor of squaring them up. To be scrappy. To drive the S-10 into scrap and keep driving it. To put what you make between you and your end. To know God and know lack and think you'll put some space between you and both. To fill a kitchen drawer with rinsed-out bread bags. To be handed bags to line your boots. To make do so long it feels like devotion. To be riled by idleness: too much television or sleep, too much time over coffee. To drink day-old coffee from a chip-rimmed cup. To brush with whatever toothpaste's on sale. To darn with cheap yarn the moth holes in sweaters. The moths come for everything. To feel satisfied when the garden's in. To fall asleep estimating the harvest. To put up seven quarts of pole beans no one particularly likes. To put up. To hear a person say *work* and swear he said *worth*. To do. To do. To abide in spareness and rarely be spared.

I've Learned to Accept

the warmed blanket I'm offered as I wait my turn.
I used to always say no. New England austerity. Aversion

to fuss. I'd wear it only briefly & I've come to understand cold
isn't the uneasiest portion. Though I'm also unlearning burden

as virtue. So I cloak the blanket over the gown that wraps
a sure slash above my left breast. When I'm told to rest

my arm on the imaging machine, I cradle it as I might have
the shoulders of a girlhood friend had I felt a greater kinship then

with my own good limbs. During the biopsy—& I'm fine
now, for now everything is fine—I soften into the nature

sounds. Bird chatter. The nurse says *A group of quail is called
a drift* & warns of the pinch. The nurse, bird lover, says *It's a weight*

of albatrosses & *expect to bruise* & a trembling—
that's finches. A quilt of eiders, plucking feathers to buffer a brood.

I propose my own: an austerity of sparrows. Nesting in exhaust
vents, roof rafters, the hard hollow of a stoplight

—& staying only for a season.
Each necessary shelter meant to be left.

Better Home, Better Gardens

The correct level of dampness for a compost pile: *wrung-out sponge*.   I compost catalogs unread

except for West Elm, from which I want three of everything. My heart is mid-century basic.   I live

in a cape, a kind of house designed in the 17th century, then revived in the 20th.   I have such a weakness for shelter

magazines. A must-have $700 cookware set? Eleven pieces and five are lids. *Ridiculous.* Tell me more.   Three experts

on the mental-health benefits of making my bed? *Oh please.* Tell me more.   If I just follow the steps

I can refinish a dresser, ferment yogurt, sew my own drapes, strip my funk-infused towels. Tell me—

Architectural Digest says a cape is quintessential summer. New Hampshire's growing season is so short.   I often dream

I'm trying to scream but can't.   I know. This is not subtle. I keep a list of ways to be better.   I keep

to the same lunch every day.   I keep thinking of things I should have asked my mom when she was alive. Remember:

wrung-out sponge.   Martha Stewart got her start at three, when she spent a day pulling spurge from the stones of a path.

Her father toed the wilting weeds, nodded approval.   Making a bed, I pull the sheets taut as a smile.   Loft the box-baffled

comforter. Let it offer what it's able.   Remember: Compost
is just useful decay.   A cape's roof is pitched steep

to help it shed snow. All that wet heft.   *Martha Stewart*
Living would list its founder's monthly chores, like *reorganize*

library and *dust all taxidermy*. Not some—all. Last year, *Living*
folded. *Dwell* is still going. Remember my cape? I love a revival.

Remember my growing season? I try to make the most of it.
Yield is its own antonym: what I produce, what I surrender.

Our Neighbors in February, 63 Degrees with No Clouds

Their friends fill the postage stamp yard and more keep coming,
bringing Frisbees and cases of Corona Light, wearing bare skin

for the pleasures of sun and being seen. They plant webbed lawn
    chairs
in the snow bank. Take turns at the grill that blooms spicy smoke.

On the second floor, hands work open a window, fitting beneath
    the sash
a speaker that thrums out "Satisfaction" and Mick leads our neighbors

and their friends in wailing from the gray-tinged snow bank,
from the porch that seems to bow under the gladness of so many
    bodies—

I can't get no! I can't get no! And our windows are open and we're
    singing it
too. Roaring about lack—though today, it's a lie.

Heliotropism

We put beans in clear cups to watch them unspool. Lengthen
toward light. This is during the worst of the pandemic,

when I homeschool the kids and teach them about living
things: turtles and mushrooms and these mottled seeds

that win us over. We give them a garden outside our window.
It's supposed to be a science lesson but I can only think

magic: broad leaves from near-nothing and each plant seeking
its pole, knowing how to tendril around it. *To seek. To know.*

I assign the vines agency. Awareness and choice. *Make good
choices* I tell the kids when I want them to wear sunscreen

without whining or pick up scattered Legos. When I take
away Minecraft, I say *Our choices have consequences.*

They want to know what my consequences are.
As a kid, I was once sent to my room for refusing to eat

our garden's green beans. My mom wanted me to just try
them. Wanted me to grow up healthy and grateful and aware

there are rules. Even so, she gave up on legumes. We've all got
to decide what merits care. Even today I won't eat green beans,

though the shelled ones I love. So maybe I turned out okay.
What I'm turning out refuses to be quantified

except for these heirloom Good Mother Stallards
with their six-seed pods, their stems trellising so densely

we can sit in their shelter. *Let's read a book here* I say.
Let's see if we can call like birds. My kids tell me *Later*, running

away with sticks, each insisting the other take
the role of the bad guy. That autumn, they'll be back

at public school, which I'll self-argue is safe
enough, and I'll cut the dried vines. Pop beans from cracked

pods and end up with a palmful. *Next season* I'll self-promise.
More light, more tending. Better Good Mother Stallards.

It's June Now

and the tomato plant, recent
seedling, has fringed itself heavy
red. It's June now,

so I've cut back the moss phlox,
deadheaded the lilacs—let
every crisped cluster settle

where it fell. Because
it's June, now the living things need
tending, more tending

than before. It's June now, my son
half done with all his childhood
summers. Month when I will turn

41, though I hardly marked May, or the year
of 40. The feeling of 35—its hard insistence
on potential. It's June, now

it's not. A day clear and clement
as that one a few Junes back.
Even dull with grief, I stopped

to shuck my sweater in the hospital lot.
It's June for now and I am wrenching
the spigot, letting the kids stir

mud in the driveway while I read
a blowsy book, transparent
protagonist and too many

adjectives. Parting pages with one hand,
a Pabst in the other, and I don't feel bad,
no—

about the blowsiness, about my lack
of doing and the once-lilacs
studding the mud. It's June. Now listen:

the Golden Sweet is unsparing, come take
some tomatoes. How could I ever
make use of them all?

Certainty

For months, heaped pallets. Then fence
rails, old barstools, armloads of brush

and with a raucous cheer they've finally
touched it off, a dozen kids ringing

its perimeter. We call these neighbors
kids though we realize they aren't—

all of them older than we were
that summer we met. Back when we knew

we knew how everything would go.
We've rolled our eyes at the ragged mess

but we have to admit this is lovely:
quiet cracking, tang of smoke. Its flicker

thickening the dark at the margins of our yard
where the last of the lightning bugs echo

the burning. Each body a beacon—
compelled to beauty, even now.

Our garden's gone quiet, save
for the asters. Fringed faces so hopeful

I should have planted a field. This hammock
curves us toward the other's comfort.

Our neighbors promise they'll see it through
to cinder—they're good kids—but they've got

all night and they're keen to keep feeding.
Fallen tree limbs gathered and accepted

with such hunger. We watch the branches go
brilliant. Take their sure chance to rebloom.

Jason Allard

Some Kind of Hero

Some writers prefer to stay in their lanes, offering readers insights to familiar landscapes. Others may well decide to pull a sudden U-turn, hop the curb and swerve through the darkest forests. Here are two very different stories. One begins on the Seacoast as we witness a neophyte reporter from Foster's Daily Democrat *settle at a kitchen table to interview a local hero. Happens every day, except Simon Lazarus just happens to be a wizard with psychic abilities who keeps rescue rats as familiars. The other is set in Japan during the samurai era as we follow a young woman named Minamoto Hikaru on a musha shugyō, a warrior's pilgrimage of revenge. What do these two works have in common? Certainly Jason Allard's skill in evoking place. And note the deft first sentences that grab the reader's attention. But more important is how the protagonists of these action stories show courage in desperate situations as they strive to do right, no matter the cost. JPK*

"I'm no hero," I said. "Never was." Sure, I was quoting a video game, one I'd spent hours playing while waiting to conduct my "interviews" for the government, but somehow I doubted my guest was familiar with it. She didn't really seem the gaming type.

"That's not what I've been hearing, Mr. Lazarus." Zoe Dyer was an intern with *Foster's Daily Democrat*, fresh from the English department at UNH. Slim, strawberry blond, pretty, with glasses over bright green eyes, and a slightly askew smile, I was sure she was a hit with young men on campus. She slid into a seat at my kitchen table, smoothed her flowery sundress over her lap, and opened her notebook. Old school. Paper and pencil instead of a tablet computer. I liked that.

I joined her, setting my steaming tea mug on the table. The breakfast nook overlooked my small herb garden. With the floor-to-ceiling windows open, droning bumblebees seemed ominously close while the air held a hint of the mint growing along the foundation.

"Merely a case of right place, right time." I plucked a small rat from my shoulder put him on the table. He settled next to my hand and scrubbed his whiskers with his paws.

Zoe leaned back, scooting away from the table, crossing her legs. She propped her notebook on one knee. I'd half-expected her at least to grimace at my animal. Skimming through her surface thoughts with a delicate magical probe, I found no fear, just a bit of surprise. Sure, reading her like this was probably unethical, and certainly illegal, but checking people around me like this was habit now, and it had saved my life a few times.

She pointed with the eraser end of her pencil. "Is that your familiar?"

"This is Enoch." At the sound of his name, the rat stopped washing his face and looked up at me. He was white, except for the small gray spot on his rump and the two gray splotches on his face, one just at the base of his right ear, the other covering his left ear down around his left eye. Unlike the pink eyes most people associated with white rats, his were dark. In the right light, they seemed to glow red.

I stroked the top of Enoch's head with a fingertip. "No, he's not one of my familiars yet. One day, maybe. He certainly has the inclination."

Zoe's pencil hovered for a moment. "You have more than one? I didn't think that was possible."

"Ask any other wizard, and they'll say you're right. The traditional familiar bond is based on willpower and domination. It's difficult to maintain with a single animal as smart as a rat. The only other sorcerer I've heard of with multiple familiars has a pair of canaries."

"How many do you have?"

"I had four. A friend gave me Grigori and his sister, Kohana. Yuki and Jojo came from a pet store."

"How did you make them familiars?"

Enoch grabbed my finger between his paws and began gently grooming me, nibbling at the nail. "It was by accident with Grigori," I said. "We were sitting on the couch, watching TV. He was on my shoulder, snuggling against my neck. The picture lost focus and the colors muted. When I stood up to bang on the TV, it dawned on me. I was seeing through Grigori's eyes."

After taking the teabag from my mug, I set it on a napkin. Enoch pounced. Without waiting for it to cool, he tore through the thin paper and lapped at the shredded leaves.

"The others took a bit more work. Rather than dominating their minds and subverting their wills, I modified the binding ritual to allow for more give and less take." I twirled my finger, directing a thin tendril of arcane energy to stir the tea as I poured in cream.

Zoe watched Enoch gutting the bag while she scribbled for a moment. "So, where did you get the idea to do search and rescue work with them?"

"While getting my Land Rover inspected, I read an article about scientists using implanted electrodes and computers to make a remote-control rat. They'd manipulate sensory input from its whiskers and stimulate the rat's pleasure centers when it went the direction they wanted.

"They theorized a rat drone with a camera strapped to its back could squirm through rubble to find trapped people faster than mundane dog-and-handler teams, or even a wizard with a canine familiar."

"I'd be curious to read it," Zoe said. "Do you remember the magazine?"

"*New Scientist*, I think."

"Is that your training area?" She asked, pointing at a large mound of jumbled bricks, cinder blocks, a few pieces of corrugated steel, sun-bleached lumber and dirt in the far backyard, amidst the wild grass and tall weeds. Beyond were a narrow strip of woods and the Cocheco River, winding its way into downtown Dover.

"Pretty good for replicating a collapsed building," I said. "Basic training was finding cotton balls hidden around the house, under furniture and such. Then we moved to burrowing through piles of fabric, and running around in the tall grass."

Enoch heard me slurp the first sip from my mug. He abandoned the teabag and stood on his hind legs. The little white rat reached up, grabbed the mug's rim and tugged. It was either coming down, or he was coming up. I lowered the mug. He stuck his face in, drinking happily.

"I imagine there was some resistance when you tried to get certified with the state," Zoe said. She smiled at Enoch.

I nodded. "Plenty. I argued with them for a few weeks over the phone. They either didn't believe my claims or didn't believe they could certify any animals other than dogs.

"I finally reached someone willing to give us a chance at their training and testing site. I think we beat the previous record by a couple of minutes."

"Impressive." She tapped her pencil on the pad a few times. "How about you? What's your background, Mr. Lazarus?"

"Homeschooled, so I was never tested for magical acuity as a kid. It wasn't until I joined the Marines anyone studied my aura closely enough to realize I'm a wizard."

Zoe scratched more notes. "I saw some of your photos. Looks like you were sent to Afghanistan or Iraq. See any action with the Marines?"

Tell me, why do you ask a question like that? I scanned her thoughts again. She was nervous, even if she did a decent job of hiding it. This was her first solo assignment. I leaned forward, furrowing my brow. "No comment." It came out somewhat flatter and a bit harsher than intended.

She stopped and looked up from her pad. I rubbed my forehead, then pinched the bridge of my nose. "I got out of the Marines and went to college before I went to Afghanistan. Studied at UNH, in fact. That's why I settled here."

"So, why were you there if you weren't a Marine?"

Oh, the things I could tell her. "Government work. I can't say who I worked for, or what I did. It's classified. Besides, you don't want to know."

She nodded. "So, what happened last Wednesday, June 6th."

My heart slammed against my ribs. I took a deep breath. "You could hear the explosion from here. The rats and I were in the breezeway, enjoying the warm air and letting our lunches settle. They lazed on a large cushion near the screen, while I sprawled in one of the wicker chairs, trying not to doze.

"From the back steps, I could see the rising column of thick, black smoke to the south, towards the Pease Tradeport. A plane, maybe even one of the National Guard's KC-130 tankers, must've crashed.

"I raced upstairs to the TV, hoping it would be on the news. Just as Channel 9 started to report, the phone rang."

◆　◆　◆

After pushing through the crowd to the yellow tape holding back the curious, I fished out my ID and showed it to the officer enforcing the thin plastic barrier. He ushered me in and gave directions to the rescue staging area at the far end of the hospital parking lot.

"Are you the guy with the rats?" another officer asked, stepping out of a knot of uniforms standing under a bright blue canopy. The name on his badge read "Capt. Dan Walton."

"Simon Lazarus, at your service," I said.

Walton showed me to a table covered in maps and blueprints, which threatened to overflow. "We were damned lucky," he said. "The plane touched down in the parking lot, crossed Borthwick Ave., and tore through this smaller building." His finger traced the aircraft's path.

"Half the plane went through the duck pond, so the fire wasn't as bad as it could've been. Then it cut across I-95 and into the woods.

"If the pilot had been right in line with the runway, he'd have only tied up the highway. Anywhere between here and there, and he'd have plowed into houses." Walton gestured. "Any further off that way, and instead of an office building, we'd be dealing with a hospital full of casualties."

I nodded. "How many victims are we looking at?"

"Like I said, lucky. Thanks to holding their annual office picnic today, most of the building was empty. We've accounted for all but a handful of people."

"Is there anything in the building I need to know about before we go in?" I asked. "Chemicals and whatnot."

Walton shrugged. "It's a processing center for a big insurance company. There may be some cleaning supplies, but otherwise it's just regular office equipment as far as I know."

"Well, let's get to work."

The charred ground at the edge of the crash site was damp from the fire hoses. I sat, folding my legs into the lotus position. Taking slow, deep breaths, tasting jet fuel and ash, I reached out with my mind. Filaments of consciousness brushed other auras. Most bristled with fear and worry, while the small ones in front of me buzzed with curiosity and concern.

My aura stretched down towards my familiars. Our energies twined together and meshed. Behind my eyelids, I could see. Colors muted, shifting away from the warm reds to the cool blues. The world exploded to life in my nostrils, a swirling chaos of unfamiliar scents.

♦   ♦   ♦

Grigori twitches his whiskers and perks up his ears when he feels the cage finally touching down. The others, Kohana, Yuki, and one-eyed Jojo, take notice was well. Grigori trots to the door and sits up, grasping the bars. His pink paws stand out from his dark fur.

Even without the familiar bond, he knows the fingers that poke through the door. He grabs Simon with his paws and begins to groom him gently, coaxing out the taste of potato chips from under his fingernails. He bruxes, grinding his teeth, and boggles his eyes at Simon, the ultimate show of ratty joy and affection.

"Ok, you know what to do. Find the survivors, and you'll each get one of these," Simon says, holding up a little white plastic tub. Grigori smells the fruity yoghurt treats inside. He presses his nose through the bars and reaches out with a paw.

Simon opens the door and they climb into his lap. Grigori jumps up on Simon's knee. He yawns and brushes his whiskers. The cute trick usually works at home. Simon shakes his head. He points at the rubble and tells them to get going.

As alpha rat, Grigori takes the lead. He heads for the wreckage in short, quick hops. The others scurry close behind him. They jump over, duck under, and dodge around all manner of interesting things. A burnt chair, a fluttering bundle of papers, just right for stashing away or making a nest with, and, most tempting of all, a plastic bag smelling of carrots and a turkey sandwich.

He stops at the bottom of the pile. He stands to test the air. Masonry dust tickles his nose. From deep inside comes something harsh and burnt. The faint stink of blood and panic. Grigori hops up the mound. Kohana and Yuki circle to the right, and Jojo heads left, keeping his one eye on the rubble.

As he climbs higher, Grigori checks each dark opening, looking for a passage inside. He backs out of one dead end in time to see the end of Yuki's pink tail disappearing into a section of plastic pipe. A faint squeak echoes out. Yuki has found a body.

Climbing over a cracked cinderblock, Grigori finds a large, dark gap under a metal desk. He waddles inside. It narrows quickly as he worms his way in. After more body lengths than he can count, Grigori comes to a wall of loose cement and plaster. Someone whimpers on the far side.

A few moments of furious scrabbling with his claws and he digs through to a void within the mound. Thin shafts of sunlight filter in through eddying swirls of dust. Inside is a smaller pile of ceiling tiles and furniture. If not for the woman partially buried here, this would have been a fun place to play. He waddles slowly towards her, squeaking. She can't hear him, but other rats will.

Answering chirps come from different directions. Grigori scrambles up to check on the woman. She moans as his whiskers brush against her bare arm. He hops onto her chest and eases towards her darkening face.

The woman doesn't react when he sniffs her cheek. He gently nips at her nose. Nothing. Her breath smells of blood. It barely stirs his whiskers. A strange, gurgling bubbles deep in her throat. He investigates her neck.

A cord, no thicker than the tip of his tail, pulls tight against her skin, nearly cutting into the woman's flesh.

Grigori can feel Simon in his mind. He will bring the other men to help the woman, but they will not reach her in time. He grips the cord with his paws and sets his sharp teeth to work.

The rubbery outer coating offers slight, but satisfying resistance. Grigori is down to metal in a single bite. The inner core has a coppery taste and his teeth tingle.

◆ ◆ ◆

The sound escaping my throat was a pale shadow of the one in my head. Even the scream Grigori unleashed when the vet gave him a shot was nothing compared to the echoes in my skull.

"What's wrong?" Walton asked. He sounded very far away and seemed to have grown to a giant's height from where I lay on the scorched grass. His offered hand pulled me to my feet.

Without answering, I shoved him aside and ran for the rubble pile. I grabbed a cinder block and heaved it aside. Then another. A couple of broken bricks. Part of a chair. It was all I could do to keep my mind clamped down, to keep Kohana, Yuki, and Jojo from falling into panic with me.

Power welled up inside my breast. It writhed through any conscious attempt at control and flowed forth, shaped by nothing more than my need to reach a hurt rat.

The ruined building erupted. Massive chunks of masonry and other debris geysered into the air as if thrown up by a titanic burrowing creature. People screamed as bricks and cinderblocks rained down. A near miss sent Walton into a hasty retreat. Within minutes, I could look down into the heart of the collapsed structure.

At the bottom, a woman coughed weakly and gingerly rubbed her throat. Grigori lay on his side next to her. His back arched awkwardly and his legs splayed out in all directions. The other rats clustered around him, nudging him with their noses and gently grooming his singed fur.

I scrambled down and knelt to scoop up my little brown rat. Jojo scurried up to my shoulder and snuffled against my ear. Kohana and Yuki climbed into my lap. I pressed my face against Grigori's belly, tears wetting fur that crackled against my cheek. I breathed in his charred smell and wept.

✦ ✦ ✦

Zoe sniffed and squeezed her eyes shut for a moment. The tip of her pencil tapped a short, staccato beat on her notebook.

"I'd have summoned a demon if it would've saved Grigori." Enoch lay sprawled by my mug, his belly full of pilfered tea. He watched me with drowsy eyes.

Zoe looked around. "Where are your other familiars?"

"They're upstairs, sleeping on my bed. This has been hard on them. Even mundane rats mourn the death of a mischief-mate. We went up to Alton yesterday, and scattered Grigori's ashes from the top of Mt. Major. I just couldn't bring myself to bury him."

"I understand," Zoe said, shutting her notebook. "Between you and Mrs. Fournier, I have enough material for this piece."

"Mrs. Fournier?"

She stood and pushed in his chair. "The woman you saved. I spoke with her at the hospital this morning. She remembered more than I expected. She's due to be released this afternoon."

My vision blurred as my eyes threatened to overflow. "That's good," I said. "Thank you."

Zoe pulled a folded piece of paper from her bag and handed it to me. "Mrs. Fournier wanted me to give this to you." As I opened the paper, she held out her finger for Enoch to sniff before quickly petting the little rat between his ears.

It was a child's crayon drawing. Most of the page was taken up by various gray scribbles. In the middle was a stick figure of a woman in a blue dress. Around her circled three little white blobs outlined in black and one all black. Each had two pink circles near one end and a pink squiggle at the other. A caption had been written with red in an unsteady hand.

"Mommy and the rattys."

Shugyōsha

"I'm going to die tomorrow, Nishiko-san," the young woman said. Outside, in the garden, the sudden clatter of the shishi-odoshi silenced the chirring cicadas for a moment. She adjusted her light yukata robe, pale blue with black mitsudomoe triskelions, and sipped hot sake. Delicate fingers brushed the back of her neck, sending a pleasant shiver down her spine, as the geisha swept aside her damp, unbound hair.

"Please don't say such things, Hikaru-dono," Nishiko said, smoothing the cloth over Hikaru's shoulders. She began to massage the tense muscles underneath.

Hikaru closed her eyes. Probing thumbs eased the knots in her back, but did no more than the hot sake for the knot in her belly. "Why not? It's likely true. Hojo Chuji is a skilled swordsman."

"Anzuru yori umu ga yasashi," Nishiko said. "Giving birth to a baby is easier than worrying about it."

"Perhaps." Hikaru drained her cup, then held it out to be refilled. The geisha's cherry blossom pink kimono rustled as she slid to the young woman's side. She picked up the steaming porcelain bottle and poured. Her movements were smooth, precise, practiced, as if they were steps of a dance. When she smiled, Nishiko's otherwise plain face glowed.

"Do not be concerned with tomorrow," she said. "There is only tonight."

Hikaru drank the rice wine in a single gulp. "Would you like to hear a story?" she asked as the geisha.

"If it would please you," she said. "I am here to entertain you. I could play the samisen, or sing, or dance if you would prefer. A game, perhaps?"

Hikaru stared into the shallow depths of her cup. "My name is Minamoto Hikaru. As a little girl, I was promised to Yagyu Gorobei. He wasn't much older, only a few years. We saw each other often, and he always made sure to say something nice to me, or give me a little present. A couple of sweets or a flower, or a little origami he'd made. By the time I was twelve, I was madly in love with him.

"A week before we were to marry, he was murdered. Drowned in the bath by three ronin after a night of playing chō-han."

Nishiko gasped, covering her mouth with one hand and laying the other on Hikaru's shoulder.

"They fled the province before we could catch them, but I was able to learn their names from the old woman who owned the bathhouse.

"I decided to go on a musha shugyō, a warrior's pilgrimage, to find his killers. My mother wept when I told her. My father was torn between fury and furious pride. In the end, he gave his blessing and my grandfather's katana. I have not seen my family in four years. Tomorrow, it will end. Either I will die, or I will take his head. Then I will return home and retake my name."

Hikaru drained her cup. "I found one of them on the road from Ise to Shima."

✦   ✦   ✦

"What's a pretty little girl like you doing with a weapon like that?" the samurai asked, gesturing at her naginata with his chin. He leaned against his spear. "You should be carrying a baby, not a polearm. Or a sword, for that matter."

"Are you Shibata Shinta?"

"What if I am?"

"Did you murder Yagyu Gorobei?"

The samurai stroked his stubbled jaw and looked up at the tall pines, swaying gently in the breeze. "The cheating whelp? It was a shame. He begged on his knees for forgiveness after stealing all of our money. Pathetic bastard got what he deserved."

Hikaru pointed her weapon at Shibata's chest. "I'm going to kill you."

The man threw back his head and laughed. "Hyakunen hayai ze!" He made a show of clutching his belly as if so much mirth hurt. "You're a hundred years too early. Go home, little girl."

She lunged forward, thrusting the long weapon. The samurai leapt back, narrowly avoiding the curved blade.

Shibata shrugged and leveled his weapon. "Very well. If you've decided to die, girl, let me help you." He jabbed at her. Hikaru danced back, deflecting his strikes with ease.

"Not bad," Shibata said.

He feinted high, then stepped in and struck low. Moving to protect her head, Hikaru was not fast enough to block his attack.

The point of his spear plunged into her thigh. Its honed edge pierced the flesh easily, scraped against bone, then erupted from the other side.

Hikaru clenched her jaw. When he twisted the spear, she screamed. She dipped the blade of her naginata, glancing it against the ground. As it rebounded, she thrust. Shibata grunted.

He staggered back, pulling his spear from her leg, and her blade from his belly. His legs wobbled, and he sagged to his knees. His spear clattered to the dusty road.

"Ikkene!" Blood coursed down Shibata's lap and spattered on the ground. Gritting his teeth, he reached for his sword. "This is no good."

Ignoring the gore flowing from her leg, Hikaru pivoted at the waist, swinging the naginata in a powerful, broad arc. Her foe curled his lip, but did not flinch as her blade cleaved through his neck. He remained erect for a few heartbeats, then toppled sideways.

✦ ✦ ✦

"How gruesome." Nishiko poured sake from a freshly warmed bottle. The rice wine steamed and filled the room with its sharp scent.

"I'd never killed a man before him," Hikaru said. "I was sick in the weeds at the side of the road, then hobbled to the nearest village, where a fisherman's wife stitched my wounds closed. I was there for three months, under the care of an old monk, with his poultices and prayers." She downed her sake. "Would you like to see?"

The geisha poured again and nodded. Hikaru pulled open the bottom of her robe. Her long, smooth legs were marred by a handful of bruises and faint scars, but one on her right thigh puckered pale and bold against her skin. Nishiko gently traced it with her finger tip. Hikaru trembled.

"Less than a handspan to the right, and I'd have bled to death before I'd taken a dozen steps," she said.

"The Fortunes smile on you, Hikaru-dono."

She shook her head. "After recovering, I headed north. I needed to improve my skill with the katana, and finally found a former ronin willing to teach me. He said I reminded him of his niece. In return for his tutelage, I fought on the side of his master against their neighbors. After several successful skirmishes, he decided to press the advantage and attack. I found the second ronin, Okubo Noburo during the Battle of Kaeru Ford."

◆ ◆ ◆

Hikaru was hungry. She couldn't help it. Last night she'd cooked her dinner in her broad, conical jingasa helmet. It still smelled of stir fried chicken and vegetables. Her stomach rumbled as the officers formed them into battle lines. The enemy soldiers did the same on their side of the river.

As the two armies faced each other, both waiting for the other to commit to crossing the river, proud samurai stepped forward from the lines to brag. They would shout their name and recount deeds done in other battles, the number of men they'd killed, or the names of particularly glorious foes defeated.

A mountain of a man shouldered his way through the enemy's ranks of conscripted ashigaru foot soldiers. His broken nose, unkempt mane of hair and grubby, stained armor marked him as nothing more than a mercenary ronin. Perhaps looking to make a name for himself and find a new lord to swear fealty.

"I am Okubo Noburo," the ronin bellowed. He waved his tetsubo over his head, a faceted, iron-studded club as tall as the man next to him. "I killed forty-seven men at the Battle of Bakaoni. At Kumoshima, I took the head of General Takeda Kenshin."

Hikaru checked the cords and straps of her light haramaki armor. It hung secure over her torso and thighs. Her hands tightened on the smooth shaft of her naginata.

Commanders shouted and gestured with their iron war fans. The two small armies advanced. The enemy reached the river first, and broke into a charge through the ankle-deep water. Hikaru and the others met them on the stony bank.

The ranks broke down quickly. Neither commander seemed to have much of a gift for the task at hand. Warriors found their own opponents to fight, either falling in the exchange or moving on to the next.

Hikaru cut down frightened, undisciplined ashigaru by the handful. The blade of her naginata became so coated with blood and caked with gore it no longer flashed in the sun. They pushed back the enemy, carrying the tide of battle through the shallow current towards the far shore.

She found Okubo standing in mid-river. Bloody water frothed around his feet. He crushed a young samurai's chest with a single blow of his tetsubo. Bones splintered with a gruesome crunch, and the man fell backwards. His wide, dead eyes stared at her.

Hikaru pointed at Okubo and nodded. He grinned and stepped towards her. Other combatants around them, understanding a challenge had been issued, sought other foes or merely stepped back to watch the mismatched duel.

"You have fire in your belly, girl," Okubo said. He shook his club. Drops of blood and other less savory bits fell into the water. "I like that."

"You killed the man I love," she said.

"Could be. I've killed a lot of men. And now, you wish to kill me. Am I right?"

She nodded.

Okubo swung his tetsubo with unnatural strength and speed. She sprang away and dodged blow after blow. He fought like an oni. Almost ceaseless brute power, but no grace. She countered every attack. Without committing to anything more than jabs and quick slashes, she could do little more than anger him.

Hikaru was unprepared when the giant changed tactics. His club, studded with knuckle-sized iron knobs, smashed the shaft of her naginata. The lacquered oak shattered. She dropped a pair of short, splintered rods.

Okubo swung his tetsubo in a murderous overhead stroke, like a workman hammering a stake into the ground. Hiraku jumped back. The club slammed down, dashing water in all directions.

She lunged forward, stepping up on his weapon as she drew her sword. Okubo released his club and backpedalled, dodging the blade slashing at his throat. He grinned and ripped his own sword from its scabbard.

They clashed again. Hikaru missed the scant safety afforded by the length of her naginata. Okubo appeared to miss the extra reach of his tetsubo.

They closed again. He stepped into his strike, straining with his arm outstretched. Hikaru skidded on the smooth river stones, trying to back away. His sword punched through the lacquered leather and thin metal plate of her armor, driving into her left shoulder.

As they parted, Hikaru slashed at his exposed arm. Her blade bit deep into Okubo's elbow. He howled and staggered back. His arm flopped like a landed fish and his katana disappeared into the murky water.

Holding her wounded limb close, Hikaru pressed her attack. Soon blood seeped from his gashed legs. A lucky blow laid open his forehead. Blinded, Okubo was an easy target as she stepped forward and rammed her sword through his heart.

◆　◆　◆

"By the time he fell, his comrades were already in flight. I went to the rear and the doctors, while the lord continued his assault. Within the week he'd doubled the size of his fief and captured several villages."

Nishiko poured the last of the bottle into Hikaru's cup. "I can't imagine an oni being as fearsome."

"I'm in no hurry to find out," she said, then drank. She shrugged open her robe, revealing her shoulders. The night air was pleasantly cooling. A faint line marked the wound. "The doctors were somewhat more skilled with their needles than the fishwife."

Nishiko leaned in close. The subtle scent of her floral perfume filled Hikaru's nose. The geisha's warm breath tickled the delicate skin of her neck.

"Very fine work," Nishiko whispered. "Hardly noticeable."

◆　◆　◆

It was still dark when Hikaru woke. She slipped out from under the covers and dressed quietly. The shishi-odoshi clacked in the garden, startling her. Nishiko murmured something in her sleep and rolled over. She began to snore softly. Hikaru smiled. Last night had been a wonderful gift from the beautiful young geisha.

She hurried, catlike, down the hall. As she stepped into her sandals, Hikaru retrieved her katana from the stand by the front door, then tucked it into her sash. She slipped out into the pre-dawn gloom.

Hikaru rubbed herself for warmth as she walked through the sleeping village. Men would be waking up soon, and heading out in their boats to fish. She made her way down to the beach, and found a rock to sit on while she waited. A hint of Nishiko's lavender perfume graced her hair.

True to his word, Hojo Chuji arrived as the first rays of the sun broke the horizon far out to sea. A pair of younger samurai, just past their genpuku coming-of-age ceremony, accompanied him. They lagged behind as he approached.

A ronin no longer, he looked well-fed and wore a brown kimono bearing the three triangle mon of the local lord and the Hojo clan. His tonsured topknot had grown gray at the temples, as had his close-cropped beard. Fine lines gathered at the corners of his eyes.

Hikaru rose and bowed gracefully. "Thank you, Hojo-san. You could have denied my request without losing face. I am truly grateful."

Chuji returned the bow, perhaps more deeply than befitted her rank. "My master advised I do just that," he said. His voice was soft, but carried over the waves breaking on the rocks and sand. "He was displeased when I told him my honor would not let me refuse. I believe I understand why you have come, and I wish to apologize."

"Apologize?"

"I assume you are the young woman Yagyu Gorobei-san spoke of while we gambled. You have come to avenge his death. I will not deny my responsibility, but I would like to say it was not my intention to kill him. I wished to offer him my services in exchange for the money he had won from me.

"Alas, I had drunk too much sake. When the other men came to force him to give up the cash, my resolve fell. I joined them in holding him down under the water, and in splitting the coins in his purse after."

He pulled a small package, wrapped in white paper, from his kimono and tossed it at Hikaru's feet. It landed heavily in the sand. "My share of Yagyu-san's money. Five koban."

Hikaru looked at it. That could buy enough rice to feed a person for fifteen years. A fortune to a ronin.

"If you defeat me, will you donate it to a temple in his name for me?" Chuji asked. She nodded.

They stepped away from the rocks, finding open space of smooth sand. The morning breeze stirred the salt air, and somewhere further down the beach, a gull shrieked. They bowed to each other again and took their places.

Chuji moved into position with the confident grace of a master swordsman. Hikaru could read his intent in his stance. He did little to hide it. The Hojo samurai would draw his sword up, and strike high with it. He would either cleave her skull, or sweep her head from her shoulders.

As she shifted her feet, there was no doubt he could read her as well. Her attack would be low, slashing at his belly, then her blade would loop around and up, over her head, for a vertical cut.

Hikaru took a deep breath, recalling the words of her sensei. "Even if one's head were to be suddenly cut off, he should be able to perform one more action with certainty." She watched Chuji, playing and replaying the motions in her mind. The first cut. The second cut. Anything else could be contemplated after. The first cut. The second cut.

Their swords flashed from their scabbards in the same heartbeat.

Matt W. Miller

Midway Through This Journey

Reflecting on parenthood, masculinity, and middle age, Matt Miller invites readers into his own life as well as those of the characters who inhabit the works of literature he teaches: King Lear *and* Moby-Dick. *With a writing style both casual and intense, Miller first conjures his classroom for us, inviting the reader to relive a single moment in a single class suspended in time. The writer next takes us surfing with his son one summer morning at Seabrook Beach. As Miller and Joe are paddling, bobbing, and planing across the waves, it is again one morning and many, as the writer balances between ambiguity and contentment, adolescence and middle age, known and unknown. The urgency to Miller's writing swells from his fierce understanding that time is fleeting, that if we're lucky, our children grow up and leave us, that his own are almost just out of reach. This thoughtfully rendered multigenre chapter, written in prose and poetry and peppered with literary references, reminds us that the imagined lives in literature help us make sense of our own. MAC*

Upon the Heath

My seniors straggle in a few at a time to the Shakespeare elective they are taking this term. The New Hampshire morning is mild for February, around 38 degrees or so, but there is snow in the forecast tonight. We are all tired at this point in the winter term and could use a snow day, but snow days are just about nonexistent in these old school New England boarding schools. Today we are going to discuss the last scene of *King Lear*, the backstabbing of Goneril and Regan, the revelation of Edgar, his battle with his villainous half-brother Edmund, and the death of a daughter and a father. We will see the old, enfeebled Lear emerge from his prison with the body of his youngest daughter in his arms, the daughter he cast out, the daughter that then took him in, in all his madness and despair and infirmity. And now she's dead too young, hung by the enemy, taken from this world, and even in his madness he must know that he is responsible.

I hear one girl, as she takes a seat at the big wooden table that we all sit around, say that the ending seemed anticlimactic. "So, they all just died?" I nod a bit. "So young, so untender," I think, borrowing from the play. I usually would not say anything; let them figure it out on their own, get into the real nuances of the scene as they discussed it together. But I am tired today. Mostly of this job. No reason to ask why. The same old reasons and all the different reasons. I suggest to the girl that maybe she read it too quickly but also that I get it, that she was trying to get the homework done, probably one of five other too long assignments she had last night. I'll give it to my students—they work hard, usually to the detriment of their health. The faculty don't do a much better job modeling balance either. By February we are all fried and just barely hauling these bags of meat we call our bodies into March break.

A couple more kids come in and fill in around the table that's covered in worn copies of a *King James Bible*, the *Quran*, the *Tanakh*, the *Upanishads*, the *Ramayana*, an old *Norton Anthology of Poetry*, *Moby-Dick*, a couple of boxes of tissues, a book about the birds of New England, a book of symbols, and a piggy bank human skull some kid used in a project years ago and that I keep as my Yorick when we do *Hamlet* and just a general memento mori. An old red '60s surfboard that my brothers and I bought for nothing in the '90s and learned to surf on as teenagers leans against the slate chalkboard where yesterday I drew a picture of Judge Holden from *Blood Meridian* for another class I am teaching. (I'll think later about that strange juxtaposition of the surfboard and McCarthy's villain, that the judge is always dancing but can that old devil surf?) This building is over a hundred years old. Thousands of kids have come through this classroom to wear out the wooden floors, bow the marble steps, and thousand more will come through, all good enough to fill a pit, to borrow from Falstaff.

"You have to slow it down," I say to the class as they pull off their coats and pull out their copies of the play. "Think about what it might mean to lose your child, to outlive your child, to carry your dead child in your arms, to know her death is on your hands, to know you cast her out and all she did was try to love you, to save you from madness and despair, to save you from yourself." It can be hard to see that on the page. I get that. And it can be hard to feel it at their age, to really feel that eternal footman Death drum his tongue across the knuckles of your spine.

"We'll watch a production," I say. "Seeing it performed helps to get closer to what's at stake. Just remember his lines when he walks on stage with Cordelia in his arms. He's not just saying 'Howl, howl, howl' and then moving onto the next line. Lear is wailing from the very core of his being, a core that's been scraped and gutted of every organ. He's been lost in dementia and now that he suddenly regains clarity all he knows is agony. How should that howl come out? How you howl comes from why you howl."

If you don't know the play, it begins with Lear, a pre-Christian king of Britain, calling a meeting to split up his kingdom between his three daughters. He is old, at least 80, and is probably aware that he is slipping in his ability to rule. I should add that this class is called Shakespeare Now and we look at plays and see how they talk to our contemporary moment. The presidential candidacies of Biden and Trump have figured heavily in our talks of Lear, which may be obvious, and will become even more obvious after the July debate that will end Biden's run. But I have also been trying to think on the personal and not just the political.

Lear loves his youngest daughter Cordelia the most and she is the person most worthy of love in the play. He has already carved up his kingdom into thirds before the play begins. Yet, as his Cordelia is his youngest, he can't give her the most without some political reason. So, he has this ceremony where each daughter has to say how much they love him.

His other daughters kiss his ass with the false pomp and hyperbole expected of such a ceremony. Cordelia, on the other hand, won't play the game. She says "Nothing" and that she loves her father "according to my bond." She loves him as a daughter should and will not embellish for ceremony, for show. "Nothing will come of nothing," Lear, her father, her king, says. He is incensed, both as a father and a king. And he is trapped. He can no longer give her anything or he loses face as a king. He casts Cordelia out. He had hoped to spend his remaining days with her and now she's gone, and he splits up his kingdom between his conniving and cunning daughters who quickly begin to whittle away his power and sense of self, gaslighting him for being old and for losing his faculties. And then they cast him out and he wanders mad with dementia and heartache upon the heath where storms rage within and without. What follows is typical Shakespeare, *Game of Thrones* type treacheries and subplots until we get to this final scene my students and I are about to discuss.

We talk a few minutes about an assignment for next week— they have to write a soliloquy in the voice of a character who didn't have one in the play, a kind of creative analysis that lets them write poetic fiction while doing a close character analysis. I tell them they can use modern vernacular if they want, even dip into languages where English might fall short for them. They seem excited about the assignment. Then, as we usually do, we start casting parts to read the scene. But I've screwed up. Now nobody wants to play Lear because I just raised the expectation of his emotional devastation. And it's Monday morning. We're all dragging a little. Or a lot. I feel as foggy headed as any Lear. I was at a writers' convention this past weekend in Kansas City where there was no lack of beer and brown liquor and early morning walks back to my hotel. I got in last night and watched the Super Bowl, more out of habit, what the bastard villain of the play, Edmund, may have called a "plague of custom," than any real interest in Mahomes winning another title or owner's box shots of Taylor Swift. Of course, I had a couple drinks watching the game with my wife and also too much meat and cheese and the game went into overtime and now I am exhausted.

I am also sad. I have not seen my daughter Delaney in weeks, not since she went back to college after winter break. It's her first year and it's been hard for me to have her gone. We talked last night on the phone about a summer job she got offered that her mom wants her to take but that she is not excited about. Too many hours for not enough money. I worry about spoiling her, but I see what she means. I try to convince her mom that $400 a week for 45 hours a week working a summer camp is not actually great money. And she needs to train for crew. And mostly she needs to have time for her art. I want her to know she should never sacrifice her art for a paycheck. In many ways I am the opposite of what my students' parents are telling them, modeling for them, by sending them to this so-called prestigious school where they live and grind each other down to saltpeter for some Fata Morgana promise of Ivy League prestige and a happy life. In many ways I am telling her the opposite of what my father told and modeled for me. And she wants to have time with us, especially with her brother Joe. Part of me knows I am being selfish because I don't want the summer to have spun by and we have not had time together. Soon she will be coming home less and less. Soon this home we have made may not feel like her home as so, so soon she begins to make a home for herself. Let's find a better alternative, we all decide. We have time, and I think she is relieved.

Still, that was last night's problem. Today's problem is that no one wants to play Lear in class. I got in the way like some meddling Polonius, who is, to quote Eliot, "a bit obtuse; / At times, indeed, almost ridiculous— / Almost, at times, the Fool." I would say that "almost a fool" falls far short.

"Why don't you do it, Mr. Miller?" a kid says. A couple of others nod in agreement. We've grown pretty tight over the last couple of months, and they are cool with me jumping in. I think. I do not like to do this, however, to take a central role in class discussion. I want the play to be theirs. Not the play I think they should see but the one they see and hear and feel for themselves. I have already said too much. I usually just do the stage directions. That way every kid gets to, and has to, do a part.

On the other hand: Fuck yeah, I want to play Lear. I miss my daughter. I feel old and addle-minded this morning. I'm no actor but I'm angry and sad about a lot of things these days, mostly my daughter leaving for college and my son drifting into his dour teenage Neverland and seeing my wife weary of my anger and sadness. I'm in the right head place to play the wrong head place. To be old and bone aching and wondering where time went.

We start the scene. Cordelia and I have been captured by the armies of her sisters. When she says we should go see them, I say "No, no, no, no. Come, let's away to prison. / We two alone will sing like birds i' the cage." I'm saying we should just go to the prison that Lear sees now as a palace, a new kingdom, where the two of them can be father and daughter again for as long as they have. It would be a palace for him but for Cordelia, young and her life yet to be lived, it would remain a prison.

I think of that time during the pandemic when my wife and son got Covid and my daughter and I had to quarantine, just when she would have been able to go back to in-person classes. She was sophomore then at the school where I teach. She'd just begun to get over the embarrassment of having Dad at her school. We had to leave the house so we would not get infected, but we couldn't come back to school until we were sure we were not. It was just the two of us for two weeks. My mom, who lives a state away in Massachusetts, owns a house near the New Hampshire coastline and so we were lucky, privileged, to have somewhere to go. We even took the dog with us. Doing schoolwork all day on Zoom. Meeting up in the evening for dinner. Walking Otis on the beach. At night we'd watch some show. Usually, it was *The*

Walking Dead because it made sense living in a bad pandemic to watch a worse pandemic. We'd follow that up with an episode of *The Golden Girls*, to take the edge off the zombie bites and barbed wire bats. Delaney was so mad at her mom for getting sick and, in her mind, forcing us to be here. The pandemic had already taken so much of her time with peers, of just being a teenager. I had to talk her down from that anger which was less about her mom and all about her not being able to see her friends. We stayed in that nice house that must have felt to her like a prison. For me, it was kind of great.

I mean, having to teach online again was shit. There's just no replacing the in-person experience of the classroom. Our school's pedagogy is student centered, discussion based. The kids lead and the teacher facilitates. But we let them go the wrong way, let them stumble through a reading or a math problem until, hopefully, they come out on the other side having not just gotten closer to an answer but how to find answers, how to think critically and creatively on their own. That's the ideal. Often it works and lots of times I just let the kids roll for a whole class without having to say much beyond, "Maybe look again at page 129" as they unpack something a character has said. But on Zoom it is too easy to check out or too hard to check in. Body language is barely existent, especially in shadowed bedrooms or crowded living rooms with hoodies over their head. These kids were back on campus and now the only online class they had was mine and they had to do it in their dorm room. It's on the teacher to set the tone, make it fun as you stare into dead lights of a computer screen. And you have to have a good internet connection.

Delaney and I were doing classes mostly at the same time and she was self-conscious of my hearing her, especially when she was taking a singing lesson. So, I did my classes in a basement room, where the connection was a little wonky at times. But it was only going to be two weeks, hopefully. I was going to teach *Frankenstein* to my 10th-graders. I set up a reading of "Rime of the Ancient Mariner" by Ian McKellen, a YouTube video a student found about galvanism and the science of Shelley's era, and some scenes from *Avengers 2: Age of Ultron*, which makes direct allusions to Shelley's story of the dangers of creating life, of playing god. I tell my students in our Zoom room, for some reason, that when you create life, you also create death. When you bring a life into a world, you also bring in their death. I try to create a sense of the immensity of parenthood and see where that hangs out in their heads as they read of Victor and his creation. Then I think of this poem I wrote years ago, when Delaney was a baby, and we were flying across the country a lot and the risk we were putting her in. It's one thing to choose to fly, or do anything of risk, but to make the choice for someone else was something I suddenly had to think about. I thought of Icarus, the child that ignored his father's advice and flew too close to the sun and died. But what a death. What a brief beautiful life. That was when the realization of her death sunk into my chest. But in the same moment I knew both this life and death were the gifts to her we could not and should not ask to take back. Here's the poem:

Club Icarus

We're no more than a few silver
seconds in the air when that winged
and cocky boy gets sucked
into a turbine sparking off a fire
that rips the starboard wing
away from the fuselage, shucking
passengers out and raining
us over northern California, dozens
of us dropping towards the bay
and you can imagine the screams,
I'm sure, the prayers cast up
then down the twirling sky,
and yet here's my daughter
laughing the whole way
down, her yellow hair whipping
around her first teeth smile,

as she titters at the tilted
wonder of what is happening,
rolling airborne over and over,
as we all drop like sacks of wet
clay and for a second I want to snag
her, to show her how frightened
she should be, so I can hug
her safe one last time, but the way
she looks laughing I just can't
and so as the brick of the bay
comes up to kiss my back I watch
my little girl giggling, grinning
floppy-cheeked into the wind
and then, damn, if I don't see, right
before the world splits my sides,
wings all her own butterfly
from her back and lift her
laughing back into the blue.

I don't share my own work with my students, and I would not read them this poem to make a point about life and death, parenting, letting your kid go to find their own life, their own death. What I do tell my students is that because our lives are so short, they are beautiful, and that is why the gods are jealous of us.

In the evening, Delaney and I would meet up, talk about what to do for dinner. Usually, I'd cook something. But sometimes, you just need takeout. Subs, Chinese, pizza. One night while we were waiting on an order of chicken wraps and mac and cheese bites, we got a delivery of flowers for Delaney. They were from her mother with a note and an apology. I knew she needed to be mad at her mom. To transfer her frustration of the last year onto something real and tangible. Emily and Delaney butted heads a lot in those high school years. Both passionate and strong women, they don't always do a good job at listening to one another. Emily acknowledges that I'm a little better, probably for having spent so many years working with teenagers in the classroom, on the playing field, and in the dorm, when they are homesick or upset about a test or game, or just in love. I've gotten good at just letting them vent and not trying to fix it, to let them find their way to an answer, like we do in the classroom.

"I'm just so mad at her," Delaney says again over the subs and macaroni bites we had delivered. Her straight blonde hair is up, she'd just done a workout for crew, as best as she could in this situation. She looks so much like me, Emily jokes. She's not her mother, just a host for my clone. And not just for her looks but in the way Delaney can take Emily for granted like I, too, often do. I can see she's still upset, but the vitriol in her voice is starting to waver. "Why did she have to go to Florida? Why did she have to be selfish?"

"She just wanted to get Nanny out of the house, out of the winter for a few days,'" I say. "She's all alone in that house. It's been barely a year since Papa died."

"I know," Delaney says. "But this sucks." It's subtle but the anger has moved from Emily to the situation. Progress. That's enough for now. I don't push further.

"Still light out," I say looking through the kitchen window. "How about a driving lesson after we are done?" She nods and we finish up. She's also taking online classes in driver's ed and needs to get her road hours in. In the car we will not talk about Mom anymore, but Delaney will wonder how Joe is feeling. She suggests we all sync up to watch a show that night.

This was a tough time for her, but it was kind of magical for me. I knew, even then, that we would never have this time together again. In a couple years she'd be in college, then off to some career, maybe a family of her own, a life of her own. At best I can hope for crowded rushed vacations together, a few snatches of minutes to catch up. But nothing like the slow deliberate hours of quarantine. I've talked to other parents since the pandemic about how, although we don't like to admit it, that there is something we miss about those days, when everyone was home, when you knew your kids were safe and within reach. We confess to a nostalgia for that time that was also so awful and filled with the terror of the unknown. Nostalgia, from the Greek *nostos* 'return home' + *algos* 'pain', to return home with pain. But there's a sweetness in that pain, in that return, that is hard to deny. It's selfish to say, but I hope one day Delaney will remember that time as a place where she got to spend a couple weeks with her dad, and she'll feel the sweet ache of what will never be again.

Now it is February almost four years later and I am Lear. Now "I am old and foolish." I read my lines slower, with fatigue. I just want to go to our cell and live in that palace with Cordelia with what time I have left. As the students read their parts they seem to pick on the energy of my lethargy. Of the tragedy. Their voices slow, their tones become darker, angrier, anxious. Lear exits as he and his daughter are taken to their prison. Edmund has no need to fear them and yet sends his captain to have them hanged, because "to be tender-minded / Does not become the sword." And then I think of something. Behind me on the mantle of the long-ago decommissioned fireplace of this old classroom, where a bunch of student art, based on books from Melville to Morrison to Alan Moore's *Watchmen* hangs, there leans a self-portrait my daughter painted in art class last year. My daughter is a brilliant artist. If I leave her with anything I hope it is faith in herself to always fight for her art. She may have bombed calculus but as long as she learns to keep that faith and fight, I will have taught her something. In the painting she is screaming, her eyes shut tight and her mouth open in a silent, Munchean wail. Around her face are cutouts of her own failed math homework and tests from high school that she glued onto the canvas. The painting is titled "Drowning."

I don't want to tell my students how to a read a scene. I want them to feel it, to feel this moment. And I want to feel it. I want the hurt of the moment coming. To know the world takes and takes but that this is why we feel so deeply and that this taking means something because we are what is taken and we are beautiful. The kids are reading their parts, even acting their parts a little, getting into their characters. I have foam swords and axes on the table, too, and Edmund and Edgar even got up to battle their fraternal battle. As Edmund dies and laments his actions, as he sends his sword with a soldier to stop the execution he has ordered, I stand up and grab the painting and hold it next to me. They are used to me getting up, so they keep on with the scene. I can tell a few of them are on to me though. When the student playing Albany, husband of Goneril, hears that Cordelia has been sentenced to execution, she shouts, "Gods defend her!" and even at this early hour she puts a little extra fervor into the lines, hoping that she can save Cordelia. She looks at the body of the slain Edmund and says, "Bear him hence awhile." And then the stage directions: *Enter Lear with Cordelia in his arms.* I emerge again as Lear. I sit back from the table, hugging the portrait of the little girl fast to my chest, pointing the picture out so the kids can see her, my daughter, my gone away Cordelia. In the picture my daughter is howling. And now I close my eyes and bellow,

"HOOOOWLLLL!!! HOOOOWWWWLLLL!!! HOOOOWW-WLLL!!! You are men of stones!!!"

Lear walks into the camp with his dead daughter slumping in his old, his weary, his worn-out arms. I yell all my sadness and anger and madness into the world. Every classroom in the building must hear me screaming, out there, upon the cold and barren heath. Some of the kids jump back a bit. A boy laughs awkwardly. And then as awkwardly, he stops. Yes, it's too much, I am being a ham, I am centering myself, my sadness, my exhaustion, but as we draw the scene to a finish, as I bemoan that my Cordelia will "come no more. / Never, never, never, never—", as I die of a wounded heart, I think I see them, my students, really seeing a father who has lost his child. Maybe they see what their own fathers and mothers might feel the moment of losing them, to boarding school, to college, to come what may. I hope this anyway, that they see what this play is about, that it is about them, these sons and daughters who we hope will know our love, despite our foolish and selfish deeds, and that we hope will have the courage to speak that love before we are all taken by the storm.

And, of course, it is about me. I have made it such. But not just because of this one class among the countless classes that have happened and will happen long after we all have sailed off into that undiscovered country. I miss my little girl. I know my daughter has not left this earth, but she has left our earth, of what was once all of us, our little family. She has not been taken by villainy—mine or her mother's or of any others. Nor by some shipwrecking storm or barbarous war. She's just off at college. She's off to start the next part of her life, a life that will have less and less to do with us, we who were once so recently all of her life. She will be back, but she will never be back the way she was, the way we once all were, a little unit of messy, noisy, goofy love. It will never go back to what it was before. And this is good. It shouldn't go back. This is how it's supposed to be. It's wonderful to feel such deep joy for her. To stand back and see this amazing woman that she has become. That doesn't mean, however, that sometimes, I am any less sad or angry. Not at what has been lost but of what has forever passed.

This past summer, before she had even left, I felt the heavy presence of leaving, of all that would be gone, changed, and irreversible. I wrote another poem, one that echoes off the Icarus poem I had written about her 18 years earlier, about negation and the inevitable presence of her absence.

Far Away

The first cold rains scurry down the gold
tipped September elms. I know

she will not be in her bedroom, a room
I realize I have hardly entered

these last few years, the door so rarely
unlocked. But walking by with a basket

of laundry for my son, I am pulled
by a thread, I think, of her perfume

adrift in the hall, her door ajar, a window
that must be cracked to the cross breeze.

I set the basket down. The white door
turns on its hinges with a whisper

of my fingers and I step through. Her ceiling
LEDs are not lit, and her desk is not

a mess of bowls and mugs, books and
oil paints. No aluminum wrappers from chips

and protein bars. Her purple blanky does
not hang at the edge of her unmade bed.

No, the bed is made. The closet, half open,
is not quite empty. And not balled on the floor,

the tie-dyed tee she so often wore to sleep.
When I catch myself in the floor length

mirror, I'm not as small as I imagined I'd be.
No, I don't look different at all. I've lost

now, her scent, that curl of flower that must
have slipped past me like a wraith,

like a breath of days spun through years,
like a rain that hushes the silence.

At times, I've a kind of proleptic nostalgia. I weep, return with
ache, for the beautiful present because I already see it passing into
memory. It's not exactly healthy, to mourn a thing the moment it
is born. My ocular trajectory is too often like that last scene in the
HBO show *Six Feet Under* where the daughter Claire is driving to
her new life in New York and as she drives, we see the characters
that we have grown to love, we see their futures, their final fate
and all of their deaths, including Claire's, who is symbolic of the
future for the show. I remember seeing that finale and crying to
my wife and having to call my brothers just in case I didn't get a

chance again. It's horrifying what the world will give us only then to take it away and keep taking. "*Media vita in morte sumus*," goes the Gregorian chant, "in the midst of life we are in death." So, on a Monday morning, sick with fatigue, with rage, with aching heart, and with age, I held a portrait of my child in my arms, and then leaned back. I howled.

Because it all is ending even as it has just begun. Already I see my students moving on, from this play, this class, from this school as they have always done, moving toward the lives they will have, the deaths they are guaranteed. And they will be replaced every year with new faces, fresh intelligence, and fresh ignorance, as they have these last 17 years, as I have moved from being Hamlet whose father is lost, to ambitious Macbeth, then into the fool father Polonius loosing and losing his children and leaning at last towards the mad and broken Lear. Already I can see Emily's great strength withering, my children scarring with all the unnatural shocks flesh is heir to, my mother joining my father, my brothers' hearts or arteries giving out, our once close knitted families scattered like some broken constellation. In Act 4 of *King Lear*, bitter and blinded as much by his bastard son as his own inability to see the truth, Gloucester says, "As flies to wanton boys are we to th' gods: They kill us for their sport." It would seem that this is true, as I howl into a Monday morning, that we are just the playthings of fate, of unfeeling gods, the tortured action figures in some cruel kid's fantasy.

But if in a moment I can step outside that howl of rage and ache and hurt, see that poor player on the stage and see that the reason he hurts so much is that he loved so much, I find something beatific. It's like the "Holy! Holy! Holy!" of Ginsberg's footnote to his own poem "Howl," the redemptive moment in the last act of the poem where the best minds are not lost but beautiful in all their suffering and kindness and love and loss. We are not the sport of gods; we are their dream. As I tell my students, our lives are short and that makes them beautiful and so the gods are jealous of us.

In one of his last seemingly salient moments, Lear will say, "When we are born, we cry that we are come / To this great stage of fools." That may be true. But there's no one else I'd want to cry with or cry for. There are no better fools than us with whom to share a stage.

Slack Tide

"The intense concentration of self in the middle of such a heart-
less immensity, my God! who can tell it?"
—Herman Melville, *Moby-Dick*

We paddled out on our boards just after dawn, my son Joe and
I, just before the low tide turned and began to fill in, making the
water too deep for waves to break over the few workable sandbars
at Seabrook Beach. It was late July in New Hampshire. A heavy
yellow-gray fog slowly moved across the water. I was reminded
of the line from Prufrock, of the "yellow fog that rubs its back
against the windowpanes." But the windows of the ocean are dif-
ferent, look inward, like Pip, the cabin boy in Melville's cetacean
epic, thrown from the whaleship, lost alone in the silent infinite of
the sea, drowning in the infinite of his soul, where he "saw God's
foot upon the treadle of the loom, and spoke it; and therefore,
his shipmates called him mad." Joe and I weren't looking into the
madness of immensity, or to see God's foot upon the treadle. We
just wanted to catch a few waves before the crowds of summer
grommets and weekend posers began buoying about on rented
soft tops and turned this break into a slalom course.

Against the sun trying to burn through the milky skyline, the
Atlantic was a slithering murky gray, like the skin of some great
eel was turning too close to the surface of the cold water. There
wasn't any land when we looked back toward shore. It was lost
in the mist. And I felt as if we were unmoored from the earth
itself, living between firmaments of air and water. I could hear
the shouts of some other surfers a little bit south of us, but I
couldn't see them. Joe was 14. I was a few weeks from 50. He
had surprised me the night before when he said that he wanted
to come along for dawn patrol. It's one thing to want to surf and
another to get up in the barely lit morning on one of the ever-
dwindling days of summer, to ride out to the coast to see if the
waves are working at all.

I was pretty fired up that he had said yes. I didn't want to push him into this thing that I loved because I knew that would be the best way to turn him off it. I'd seen it happen in him with other sports and other hobbies, things he had shown an initial interest in but then had ebbed. If the love happened at all, I wanted to let it come to him naturally, like a tide coming in. I got up before he did that day, in the bruised colored dark, to throw our wetsuits and boards into my car, make myself some coffee, and make him some breakfast—a bowl of cereal and some chocolate milk. The ride from Exeter, where we lived, where I taught English and sometime coached football, and then through Hampton and over the channel bridge to Seabrook, takes about twenty minutes. We were quiet the whole ride, the jazz station playing softly, like when I drove him to school most mornings.

About two miles past the bridge, we turned left on Newbury Street where my mom owned a house and where I always knew I could park, away from the summer crowds at the more parking lot accessible beaches. We pulled into the pebbled driveway and got out to check the waves. I could hear them crashing even before we crossed over the dunes, and I got a little pinch in my gut. The sound of the waves was being carried on the onshore breeze. Onshore breezes can hurt the shape of waves, knock them down from behind into walls of foam instead of the curling barreling glassed-off faces surfers hope to see in wave checks and waking dreams. So much depends on the whims of the wind and the wind is a product of the sun, a child of the sun, and really, when we surf, as Daniel Duane writes in *Caught Inside*, we are really surfing sunlight. It's that light you want to see, caught in the curl of the wave, as you come over the dunes. But I had my doubts with this fog and with this breeze.

I said nothing to Joe. He may already have been thinking the same thing, already in doubt about why we were here, if it would be worth it. But maybe he was thinking about something else, about some game he'd been playing on the PlayStation or maybe high school starting in the fall. If he was thinking about the wind, he didn't say so. He didn't say anything. Joe, being a fairly reticent kid by nature, usually doesn't. That's fine. There's a lot of quiet in surfing, especially at dawn. Maybe that's why Joe likes it. No coaches hollering, no manufactured "rah-rah" spirit, no parents in the stands clapping and whistling for you to hit, catch, or throw some ball. Even when you paddle out with friends, you are still on your own, looking out into the looming, and back into the self. On big days, even if it the lineup is crowded, there's a quiet humming above the roil of waves, a nervous silence broken softly by the far away hoot of someone stoked by the pull of a wave's slate shoulder.

Joe's a teenager in a different world from the one I knew, where we couldn't get out of the three station TV house fast enough in the summer and wouldn't come home except to raid the fridge with our friends before cockroaching back out to skate or play hoops or Relievio. Or you'd wander by yourself on a bike or a board looking for where your friends were and not really caring if you found them as you wandered through your own head. Joe's is a world ever asking kids to be noisy, to shout on social media, to brand themselves, to be, if I borrow from Emily Dickinson, "public as a frog."

It's not news that social media and constantly being plugged into the noise of the world is not great for any of us. It's especially bad for kids. In *No Country for Eight-Spot Butter-flies,* Julian Aguon writes "the only way to make the successful journey (from adolescence to adulthood) is to learn how to 'get quiet'—that is, to quiet down the noise of other people's opinions and to take instructions instead from one's own heart." Joe seems to have a good instinct for getting quiet and listen-ing to himself. I don't always find a way to get quiet, to find what my poet buddy Willie Perdomo calls the dream space, that place between all the noise rushing in, all the noise that wants to rush out. Except when I'm out in the water. That's where I can get quiet. Dwell within. Breathe. At the beginning of *Moby-Dick,* Ishmael says that the sea is his substitute for the pistol and ball. "As everyone knows," he says because of the damp, drizzly November in his soul, "water and meditation are forever wedded."

We came over the dunes, into the brimming sunlight, as migrating monarch butterflies flitted above the high dune grass. We were both of us still in street clothes, our hoodies up. We walked all the way to the water just to look at the waves. They weren't great, not the polished mirror-faces an offshore breeze would shape them into. Mushburgers I might call them, in that surf vocabulary you acquire over years of doing this, a language Joe does not have yet. Still, with waist-high peaks there was a little size and push to them, and it looked like, through the drifting mist anyway, that some of the set waves were lining up and even walling up a bit on the inside. For July, July in New England especially, it wasn't bad. And the water was pretty warm, thanks to that onshore breeze pushing warmer water to the coastline even as it junked up the waves.

"What do you think?" I said to Joe, not taking my eyes off the waves, knowing, like me, he was also staring hard into the brightening fog. Was excitement starting to build like little flecks of lighting across the back of his neck? Nervousness? Disgust? His expression was as granite as the state he was born in on that howling December night two days after Christmas, and almost exactly a year after my dad had died.

"Yeah," is all he said. Then I did look at him, in the periphery. He'd gotten so tall in the last year, close to six feet and pushing 150 pounds, the same size as me at the same point in life, right before high school, right before I started playing football and turned away from surfing and skating for close to a decade. His head was a mop of sun-bleached blond hair. The line of his jaw was strong, no longer that little guy who would bury his puffy cheeks into my chest when he was tired or sad or had just had "too much." I recalled a day last fall when we were watching TV on the sectional couch in the living room and he slowly leaned back into my chest, something he used to do so easily but had not done in so long. I knew then that it was probably likely the last time he would do that, that he would feel it okay to snuggle back into his dad. I wonder why this intimacy fades? Is it cultural or biological? Do we teach that there is something wrong about this kind of tender touch between men or is it just a natural progression of adolescence, a need to pull away from the father, the parents, as one begins to claim their own self and identity? I can remember being a toddler lying on my father's chest and the last time I hugged him before he died. But in between those moments there is little that is tender. When I go real dark, I fear that maybe the next time Joe leans into my chest is to check for my last breath. But I wasn't thinking that then. I was thinking how he looked a lot like me now, sounded just like me in pitch and cadence and that monotone mumble I pass off as speech. But he was not like me at that age, so full of self-doubt, lacking courage and conviction to be himself. Or at least this was what I thought. Shit, maybe I just project some idealized state of being on him. Whether I do that for him or me, I'm not sure. He at least seemed surer of himself that I was at that age. As much as he looked like I looked then, I didn't want him to be me.

We turned and we went back down the road to the car. Then we tugged into our wetsuits and got our boards. I thought about taking out a longboard since the waves were on the small and crumbly side. I decided instead on this quad fin mid-length I picked up near the end of the Covid lockdown, back when ordering stuff online was a balm to bottomed-out spirits. Anyway, it was something that works well in small or big waves, a kind of a stretched fish, a little wider and longer than a shortboard. It paddles into waves easy and has enough planing to make the next sections of smaller waves like these without having to do all the ass wiggling needed with a shortboard. But it still moves and will let me crank some cutbacks, as much as my aging body is up to on a given session. Joe used his Torq. This board has a pointed nose and a bit of rocker, which is the curve a surfboard has from tail to nose. A lot of rocker allowed for more maneuverability but made it less steady and harder to ride for an inexperienced surfer. It also had the thickness of a longboard through the middle making it much easier to paddle and pop up on, even it's a bit stiff when it comes to turning and carving. It was a solid, not too expensive, factory pop-out first board. Good to learn on. He and his cousin Jack had both got one a couple of summers ago but were now starting to progress past them.

Yanking my suit over my head and beginning to rub some wax on my board, I realized I was in a hopeful, even happy mood. It had been a while since I'd felt like this before a surf. Lately, I'm all by myself during wave check, staring out at sun coming up over the water, squinting to see what sandbars or reefs are working, how crowded the lineups are. I surfed alone a lot these days. The mixed crew I had surfed with the last couple of decades weren't around anymore or just weren't surfing. My buddy Dave, who I've known since 7th grade, who got me into surfing, was living with his family in Portugal, probably bodysurfing Lagos or Esposende. His brother Justin had moved back from Hawaii a few years ago but had mostly quit after breaking his back in those heavy waves and probably had little patience for the mercurial and frigid waves of the North Atlantic. McGuirk died when we were in our 20s, flipping his car into a dumpster one night racing home drunk from the Whipple. Vinny was surfing but I didn't see him out there much since his contractor business put us on different schedules, and he had his son to surf with now. Philibosian's brain cancer and recovery took a lot out of him but not as much as a messy divorce and a nasty child custody battle. My pal Ralph had retired from teaching and was spending more time with his grandkids, his guitar, and his boat down in the Cape. Whole thing feels like a sad middle-aged Jim Carroll song. I had said to my wife recently that I thought I'd be surfing with my kids by now. But Delaney, as much as she loved being in the water and would spend hours playing in the cold waves, who would be off in the fall to row in college, never quite caught the surfing bug. Not yet. And lately Joe had seemed to be going inward, away from everything and everyone, like so many teenagers do, like I did at his age. I like to think it's the great long silence of drawing in a breath before speaking the world into existence. And I worry that the words will never be found.

So, it was nice to have someone else to paddle out with. We didn't have to talk, just exist in a parallel space, knowing someone else is there, that neither of us are alone. As we paddled out, me and my kid digging toward the fog and a murky horizon, I was elated, little cracks of lightning rolling up the knuckles of my spine. I must have had a shit-shining grin on my face. But I was also nervous that he might not have fun, that he was just doing this for me, that if he got wrecked a couple times he might just paddle in, sink into some video game on his phone in the car while Dad bobbed in the surf, looking like a lone and lost seal in his wetsuit. He got worked pretty bad one time last summer while out with his cousin so I thought he might have had enough with surfing at all. But here he was, jumping on his board to paddle out with Dad.

He hadn't been out in bigger waves in a while and since it was low tide it was going to be a long paddle out, meaning we'd have to get past the rolling beach break that was plowing in toward shore. Luckily the air was warm and water was a practically balmy 64°. Paddling out in the winter when the air is 20°, the water 40°, when each wave spikes an ice cream headache through your skull as you beard crystals in the wind, is another story. But getting caught inside, meaning when you're caught between the shore and the break line, can be a crushing limbo of paddling in place for twenty minutes. Even in the summer it sucks. And if you're middle-aged like me, a little too symbolically on the nose. To get out quickly, it helps to know how to duckdive, to dip the nose of the board under the coming wave and let its buoyancy push you up and out through the back of the wave without losing any momentum. It took a mix of well-timed grace and subtle strength. I gave him a quick tutorial as we paddled out, hoping he'd pick up from my example.

"It takes practice," I said as he got pushed back a couple times. Duckdiving is one of those things, like a lot of things, like love and parenting and poetry, where you learn by going where you have to go. So he kept paddling out, getting washed back here and there, until he got past the break point.

Now we were bobbing, half submerged in the dark water, half swallowed in the catfooted fog, waiting for a set. The water, moving like swirling moleskin, was warm for this time of year. It seems to be getting a little warmer every year. When we saw a big gray seal poke its head up not far from us, curious maybe if these black forms floating nearby by are some sort of brethren, I thought about how more and more common these bigger seals are in these waters, as they chase the cooler northern temperatures. And if they are more common, so are the great whites, those nictitating Grendels that feed on the fat of seals, and sometimes show a gnashing curiosity about surfers. The shark sightings and shark attacks that have started to be so common on the Cape in recent years had begun to creep their way up in lateral undulations to New Hampshire and Maine. My fishermen friend Eric told me about an app he has that tracks all the great white activity in the world, including these waters off the coast of New Hampshire. I don't have that app and I don't want it. One time my buddy Dave and I were out surfing at dusk and something long, dark, and dorsaled swam between and below us as we waited for a set to come in.

"You see that?" he said.

"Nope," I said.

"Me neither," he said. There is a faith that only willful silence creates. And what is that line Ishmael utters as he enters Father Mapple's church and sees the names of sailors lost at sea written on the walls, "faith, like a hyena, feeds upon the tombs"?

Joe and I were not thinking of what lurks below. The first wave came in, its peak closer to Joe. He turned and paddled into it, popping up smoothly and taking a good angle to make an okay right, skimming down the line as I watched and hooted from behind. It was the first time he had caught the first wave whenever we had gone out together. A sign of what's to come, I thought. At some point, I will be watching him from the beach, shoulders and knees too arthritic to go once more unto that breach. Then I thought, get over that maudlin shit and paddle for a wave. Before I could, Joe caught the second wave. He glided nicely down the face, instead of just riding the foam forward like most less experienced surfers do. He'd been summer surfing for a couple of years and was starting to get consistent at angling the board as he paddled and popped up so he was in the pocket of the curl, that whorling engine of the wave, with the glassed-off face of the wave ahead of him. He steamed down the line and I could see he was just starting to figure out how to use his body to glide the board up and down the wave. Then I paddled into a chest-high wave of my own, dropped down across its face, cutting back up towards the lips then back down to tuck into what little barrel there was before skimming off the fading shoulder. Not the greatest wave but enough for a New England summer stoke.

Joe wasn't ever much into team sports, the ones with coaches and players shouting and yelling and clocks and points and all the chest-pounding and ass-slapping that goes along with it. He'd played soccer and flag football, but nothing really stuck. He'd been getting good at baseball and we would go out to take batting practice and shag balls on his free days after school to get better. But then Covid came and killed that interest. Maybe his interest was more about trying to do well for me anyway. Hard to tell and he won't say. Not yet anyway. I got it, though. I had a hard time abiding some of that stuff too. For some there is a joy to all of it that comes natural and good for them. I liked the fierceness and focus I found in silence. I think the helmet might be why I liked football more than other organized sports. I could keep my mind private inside that space, even as my body ran around blocking and tackling, even as I ran drag routes across the middle of the file to snatch the ball out of the air knowing a middle linebacker was about to crush me like a nor'easter heavy wave might pound me into the infinite grave of a January Atlantic. There was something like being inside a tunnel of water about it, if that makes sense, a little bit like being covered up inside the barrel of a wave.

Joe had always been surer of himself, more deliberate, than I ever was and has never done something because it was expected of him. His will seemed his own, which was admirable. It can also be frustrating, like when you get the whole family to some restaurant for dinner, and he didn't bother to wear or even bring shoes. Or we'd be all fired up to do something, like go see some new MCU flick, and he would decide he would prefer not to, like some tween Bartleby. Of course, all of this could be me misreading him but his quiet truly seemed to come from a confidence in himself. My quiet at his age came from terror. He'd do something if asked and he would do it well and then be on his way. But he would never cave to social pressure. If all his pals were getting together somewhere but he wanted to go up to his room and draw or work on his digital animation projects, he would. No FOMO in Joe. Not one to be swept up in the current of social expectations peer pressure, he'd just swim out of the rip and into his own current. Again, I go back to Melville, *Moby-Dick*, and the sermon where Father Mapple says, "Delight is to him—a far, far upward, and inward delight—who against the proud gods and commodores of the earth, ever stands forth his own exorable self." That's why I always asked if he wanted to go surf, never made him like I know some surfer dads, baseball dads and other sports dad do. His life, his choice. Now to watch him glide across that wave of his own will was just beautiful. His lean grace and athleticism seemed to flower out of that whispering hush of rolling water even as the fog softened and obscured his shape.

Then he pulled out of the wave and started to paddle back from the blur. I saw him grin his little grin. He doesn't smile much so when he does it can be everything. My chest filled with what felt like a light. I wanted to do this with him forever. And in the middle of my elation, because of where my mind always goes, I felt some ache of loss. I started to wonder how long I could do this? How long could I keep coming out into these waters with my son? I was a better surfer than Joe but not for long. My back, my knees, my shoulders, and elbows, will start to go. Have started to go. I've already had one ear drilled because of exostoses, or surfer's ear, bony growths in the ear canal caused by cold and wind and sand. I have a fracture in my elbow from football that balloons with bursitis every once in a while. When will melanoma catch up with me? When will a valve shut down in my heart? Or an embolism explode in my head? I hope I'm in the water when it happens and not drooling in the slant of a midafternoon light wearing rolled-up pajamas.

Swamped deep in middle age, half-way to a hundred, an age I was unlikely to reach looking at how few of the men in my family made it out of their sixties, I bobbed half out of water, half out of air, watching Joe. He was still a kid, but in most ways, he was no longer a boy. He was 14, halfway to adulthood, or at least to the point in our culture where adulthood demands really start to kick in. We are both somewhere in the median, both of us. Physically, his body was exploding out its pupal stage. Mine was pulling back in, toward that final chrysalis of the grave, after which who knows what form we find, if any. His tide was rising, the world about to open up in so many ways. I wanted so bad to be there for it even as my own tide was pulling out, as the current pulled me toward slow diminishment and some untouchable, unknowable horizon. We were both living in two worlds, or between two worlds—Joe between boyhood and manhood, me between my meridian and death. We were like Melville's whale, something that lives in the water but breaches toward heaven to breathe the air. Of multiple worlds and no worlds. Perhaps that is the Cartesian state of all of us, here but also not here.

And now writing this, I think back, not of the boy Pip, adrift in the silence of self and sea, but of old Captain Ahab. In "The Symphony" chapter, he looks out over the horizon line of the sea, thinking on his own young son back on shore and feeling his own diminishing against the horizon even as he pursues his whale and his fate. Early in the novel he told his crew that "All visible objects, man, are but as pasteboard masks. But in each event—in the living act, the undoubted deed—there, some unknown but still reasoning thing puts forth the moldings of its features from behind the unreasoning mask. If man will strike, strike though the mask."

Now, in this later chapter, he almost seems resigned to not knowing, to letting go of his rage and ruin. He is 58, in the between of middle and old age. He is hunting this whale because he needs to know whether the wound he carries, the life he has lived, was random, entropic, or ordained by the universe, guided by some God, some handspike of fate. In the end he cannot live in the doubt of am I or am I not, in the in-between, in this place where he doesn't know for sure what has come before, what lies ahead. "That inscrutable thing is chiefly what I hate," he told his crew when they shipped. He needs to know, and that drives him mad. "Is Ahab, Ahab?' he asks. "Is it I, God, or who, that lifts this arm?"

The confusion of adolescence, the confusion of middle age, maybe they are not so different. We want to know what's next and are made mad in our agnosia. But perhaps being willing to live in the doubts, to be able to function and thrive despite not knowing, perhaps this is where some faith in one's path is most profound.

I'm framing middle age as its own kind of adolescence, some dip into light, newness, even brilliance of potential. The body is changing, aching, the mind is changing, aching, and everything is uncertain. A second ago, I was king of my playground, had confidence with the game I was playing of work, art, and family. But now I know less than I ever did. Joe does not talk much, there but not there in so many ways, that same pyramidical silence Ahab senses in the whale. At times I feel like I lost him long ago, like I did too much or not enough and now there's no way to reset that. I have no idea what to do now. I am sad and terrified about what is fading away.

But isn't that like growing up, leaving behind the toys and games you used to play? I am looking into the unknown future even as I'm heading into fifteen again, into high school again. I have no idea what's coming next. Could be cancer. Could be prizes for poetry. Could be walking my daughter down the aisle or watching one of my brothers try to come back from a stroke. It's all these things. It's all out there and there's also nothing out there. All the beauty and all the terror await. And there's nothing certain but uncertainty, doubt. And the question is how to live in the doubt, how to navigate the ecstasy and agony of what happens and what may happen. I'm in the middle again, "the right path lost," as Dante says on the cusp of hell. I thought I used to know things, used to believe that the mind "Can make a Heav'n of Hell, a Hell of Heav'n" or so said Milton's Satan.

Now I know nothing. Even as the rip pulls me into the unknown. Will I go to it maddened as Ahab? I like to think that I'd be like Flask, third mate on the Pequod, an attendant lord, a butterless man, caught between labor and management, when he said, "I know not all that may be coming, but be it what it will, I'll go to it laughing." That's a fool's wisdom we hope to have when we face the abyss of the infinite.

As Joe paddled back out, as he still clumsily but ever more effectively duckdived oncoming waves, I felt (or imagined I felt) the tidal current slow, even stop, as if it had paused to listen to this moment of the earth. When Joe reached me and sat up on his board, there was no wind, and the fog just hung like a curtain of heaven, the waves rolling out of the infinite toward us as we floated on the littoral lip of the Atlantic. I felt at once both the immense profundity and insignificance of this moment, a dad and his son, just floating on fiberglass, our toes baiting the biting maws of the chthonic below us, our backs to the things on land that will try to consume us, our eyes watching for a pulse of energy on the water. Supplicants to the indifferent sea and sun, we said little. We got quiet, drawing breaths, and so maybe we said everything we needed by being here together in the middle distance of our lives.

There is a point in the movement of ocean called the slack tide, when the water is not really moving, is not coming in or going out. It's usually brief, a flicker, a moment of motionlessness, not receding or advancing, of existing in some sublime in-between that you don't even notice except, sometimes, when you do. Now in the middle of everything, between water and air, between quiet and the crashing of waves, between the thick haze and the morning sun trying to burn it off. I stopped thinking about all that was behind us, all that lay ahead of us. I dialed into right now, into each stroke of my arms, each peak beginning to feather toward break, each drop I made into a wave. And I watched Joe do the same, planing across the unfurling scroll of water, the waves taking him from me as he slipped from my sight into the mist.

John Perrault

Whatever You Got Going On

The twenty-one poems that John Perrault has gathered here are clustered in groups of three, like separate movements in a musical suite, each unfolding with a different theme. One can't help but admire this poet's formal skills: his subtle rhymes and half-rhymes, his use of consonance and assonance, his mixing of enjambed and end-stopped lines to vary the flow of his words down the page—all of which he harnesses to render his emotions and thoughts through vivid imagery. In this Perrault is a master, as when he describes the "unorthodox calm" he sensed during a canoe ride at dusk. "So strange it is—this stillness. To be here, / in a patched canoe, watching myself down there / beneath the surface, not moving a muscle. / Not sinking into a funk. Suspended in air." In poem after poem, his precise language suspends us there, too, beside him. RF

> *And so, let us walk the path, dear friends,*
> *ever conscious wherever it ends,*
> *it may very well be our beginning.*

Hill, Milton & Wright

Geoffrey Hill's most likely right,
but I'd just as soon be wrong.

Just as soon be reading Wright
as skimming Milton. Milton's
Master, don't get me wrong. But,
as Lightfoot said, the feeling's gone
and I just can't get it back.
Watching Lucifer wing his way
down the light, around the dark,
back up and into the sun
strains the vision. Things start to blur.
I mean, poets go blind staring
into space like that. Give me
a pasture in Minnesota,
a little twilight, a black
and white pony to nuzzle
my left hand, and I'm in heaven.
Hill would give me hell, no doubt,
but I can't help reaching to stroke
that wild mane. Caress that long ear.
So yes, I'm bound to follow Wright
"along the sweet path he cut
through the dryness." Right behind
Mary Oliver I go,
whose words these are I think you know.

Early Morning Rain

"I know that song," she said,
"but don't look at me when I sing."
He looked at her: Not smiling,
serious . . . maybe a little sad.
"Okay," he said, turning
to the window, running some chords,
tuning a string. "Weathered words
to this one. Ready?" She said nothing.
And they began—softly
at first—her third floating over
his lead, her voice rising clear
as a Deerfield pond. Sweet harmony.
What is it about song?
Like we're all tangled up in blue.
Like we haven't got a clue
what our hearts have to say till we sing.
Outside, the all-day rain
was letting up. Bit of light mist,
breaking clouds. "The sun at last,"
he said, and turned. Her eyes were shining.

For the Birds

I, too, was of three minds.
Either/or was out—
a trinity of doubt I was,
about to do nothing
given everything.

Easy for me to say
how easy for you
facing but this—but that. But then
you only need choose…
You'll have to excuse me.

I was beside myself.
Me here—me there—
me watching myself giving
up on the guess of which
mind not to follow.

There was the swallow
darting through thin air,
there was the jay pecking hard ground,
and then there was that crow
in the lilacs—laughing.

> *Who's that standing stern at the gate?*
> *Who is it hates to give in?*
> *Whose words—whose lips—burning?*

The Piano

A cottage left for winter can be rough—
cold scuffs the floorboards in the hall,
the walls creak and shiver with the wind,
and closet doors tend to click, unclick,
as if trying to latch on to something
close at hand but can't connect.

In the cupboard, thank god, the bottle
didn't freeze. Icicles rattle
in my glass. I pass the salted windows
wrapping every room except the den—
dark as ever—yet in the mirror
on the mantel, my children swim.

The upright in the corner wears a sheet
of white, the angels in the photograph—
wings. I pour another scotch, spread
my fingers out to find the key of C
for "Silent Night" and sing it flat.
No matter, nobody here but me.

The Conversation

From my long walk around the point
over the high crags and shingled beaches,
over the slick outer boulders
edging the low-tide lip of the bay,
I hiked back with a pair of cold stones,
one in each of my trouser pockets.

Gray with garnet threads, and worn away
to smoothness by tumbling in the sea for eons,
their surfaces were comforting to touch—
they felt as if made for human hands
to hold, for human palms to weigh them,
warm them, with fingers closing round.

I handed them to her without a word
about our argument—about my taking off;
she placed them on the table by the lamp
and turned away—then she turned again.
We pulled up chairs to study them together.
Waited. And the stones broke the silence.

The Blue Hood

"So what," she said, "if dead leaves lie on the moss
like that?" "So *what*?" he said. "So what," she said,
"just that—too late for this." And it came to pass
that as he raked, he fumed. And as he fumed,
it began to snow. Light. Whispery. Red
oaks took on the glow of age-old lichen.
The snow thickened. Dusk thickened. And he found
himself talking himself to a calm, raking
what he could before hauling in the wood
she wanted. He half-hummed an old carol
to a tree, stuck his tongue out for communion
with the snow, pulled off a ragged mitten
to clear his eyes—turned—squinted: spotlights flooded
the frozen ground. Heavy doors slid open.
She angled toward him down slope from the barn,
zipping up her jacket, fiddling with her hood.
"I can't seem to get the knot out," she said.
"Let me try," he said. "You look good in blue."

What peaks lie ahead
in our oh so restless hearts?
How steep the ravines?
How deep the water?

Up On the Border

I leave the lake
to hike the blue mountain.
My heart is full.

Flush with berries,
the thicket takes my hand
and won't let go.

In the Laurentians

Snow—and hush of winter;
the moon's a silver slipper in the sky,
and the stars—blinking bits of glass
frozen in our eyes.

We have our toboggan,
our mittens, jackets, hats—we have our hearts.
What's fur between the two of us?
What is it that hurts?

We work our way over
the edge and drop, eyes blurring in the wind.
Eyes blurring, flying down the night
into the last turn.

Fifty odd years ago…
Ice shags the firs tonight. And there's the moon.
I call your room and you answer,
still on the wing. Still holding on.

And now you're gone.

Poem Beginning with a Line by Tomas Tranströmer

The canoe glides out over the water,
the bow points west, into the last of the light.
Two loons divide, either side of the gunwales,
dive, and are gone. The lake is long. I have all night.

I have all the stars to work the figures.
Thoreau's question: how much will it cost my life?
The hustle, the chase, the nose to the grindstone.
Now, this unorthodox calm. This disbelief.

I ease my paddle aboard, let it drip
into my boots, close my eyes, lip the word "peace."
Is that what this is? I take a healthy swig
of beer, lean over the side, stare into my face.

So strange it is—this stillness. To be here,
in a patched canoe, watching myself down there
beneath the surface, not moving a muscle.
Not sinking into a funk. Suspended in air.

I can just make out my tent at the edge
of the point. A black smudge angled toward the cliff.
In the back-lit sky, three feathery pink clouds
pool their colors. Deepen. Bathe me while I drift.

Let us stretch the canvas taut,
mix our colors,
step into the frame.
Let us make something…

Northern Point

after Wyeth

Gray granite ledge
edging out rippled sea.
Dry salt-sifted grass.

Amber orb—rod
rammed through parched peak of roof.
Shadows. Shakes. Cracks. Chain.

Hard Maine, stone cold,
honed by sand, wind—landscape
primed for the taking.

Landscape claimed by
tempera on gesso.
Back to bone. His point.

Gustave Loiseau

There's an early summer scape,
a bit lush, with powder puff clouds,
lavender trees, leaping green grass,
pink horseshoe path, blue stones, ruddy hedge…
Is it the heat that turns him on?
Or is it me?
But come the deep winter,
houses snowed in at Pontoise,
drifts blocking doors,
his brush finds just the right edge
to handle the cold. Critics like him.

Son of a Paris butcher,
he didn't make the cut. Liked to paint.
Liked to work en plein air—
maybe catch sight of Gaugin, Bernard,
up at Pont-Aven. Went to the cliffs,
the rivers, the woods. Mist over
water meant everything to him.
But what? (If you canoe
you know the answer:
Silence. Drift. Wait. Not a word.)
He won't say because he can't. Like you.

Paint can ignite when you're young,
working too close to the flame.
Over time you back off.
Over time you embrace your doubts.
I'm standing outside the frame
of his house in Pontoise, leaning
in for a look. Anybody home?
My eyes are watering. I'm cold.
The Artist invites me in.
It's warm inside looking out
while he works. An old man now. Like me.

Connoisseur

for Peter Agrafiotis

Peter's painting clings to the dining room wall
in a gap between windows: two grass huts
perched on the edge of a peak in Nepal.
It stops our company quick in their tracks,
cuts right to the giddy question: are they here?
Or there? So luminous the light breaking
over the crags, so surreal the faint fear
of falling. If a finger's touch has shaken
their equilibrium, the point's not pressed.
They study the worn rug beneath their feet,
the wine glass in their hands. Besides, Frank's guest
has pulled her pinky from the paint. She's petite
but she can holler: "We saw the original
at the Met, right Frank? Right Frank? Incredible!"

> *The exploited ones, enduring ones,*
> *lifting their song from the earth,*
> *singing for all it's worth the fact of their lives.*

Buddy Bolden

> *This music begins on the auction block.*
> —James Baldwin

When Jefferson purchased Louisiana
it was a dandy of a day. Napoleon's
Prefect stuck a finger in the air to test
the weather, counted up his francs, bought drinks
for all the drunks along Toulouse, hauled down his flag,
handed back the quays, shoved off and shipped south.

No doubt about it people, history
making in the making—shaking out the map.
Now we're talking elbow room—now we're talking
double down the trade. Crack in the Constitution's
all it took—little wiggle room—little wedge of words.
Chisel just slit enough to slip a dollar through.

And what a night to party: sickle moon
silvering the rigging in the slavers,
fiddles flying, tearing up the Vieux Carré—
creoles dancing the calinda, the chica,
slurping down the gumbo, sloshing down the rum,
poking fun at the baby-faced Yankees on parade.

And on the Place d'Armes, underneath the colors,
cornered by the chaos of the crowd: King Bolden's
great granddaddy, buckled to a buckboard,
shouldering a chain, holding on to nothing
but his heart—sucking in, blowing out, cutting
one last Mississippi solo to the bone.

Foreclosure

Deer sidle into the yard at midnight
for the blackened acorns under the snow—
they watch them from the kitchen window.
Last winter two, maybe three. This year, eight.

Seven does, a buck, working a good foot
down to scratch a living—nosing dead leaves,
frozen grass, small chunks of brittle moss,
for what they have to offer: Bitter fruit.

They sit in the dark with only the lamp
across the road for light. The buck circles,
stakes claim to a patch up by the fence—
a doe approaches, backs off with a limp.

Neither stirs, says a word, when the last deer
moves on. When dawn defaults to a gray sky
marbled with gold. When the clock strikes eight,
and the Sheriff arrives with the papers.

Bag Lady, Christmas Eve, Manchester, NH

"No room, sorry," says the clerk
to our lady of little means
whose social security seems
to hinge on best wishes.

Clerk's a stiff—why she slushes
her cart down Hanover, up Elm,
cross Lowell, now back—find a home
for the night. Getting dark.

Some frosted entry—awning—
baby Jesus in the window—
little lamb. Mary there? Peek through
the double-plated glass.

Jim's Men's Shop. My good god yes.
Lord thank you Jim—for this manger,
those sheep, shepherds, angels—that star.
Just about everything.

And here's everything she sets
in his doorway: bags, blankets, mat,
book, half a ham sub, can of Pabst,
chips, and—for what it's worth—

a little peace on god's earth
for this one night. Tonight, my friends,
that clerk can take his half-ass inn
with no rooms and shove it.

The least one can do is face what is true.
The least one can do is do something.

The Times

The old barn looks like it's burning
as the sun sparks the morning frost
coating the sheath.

It smokes outside the kitchen window
while the shingles shrink and curl
and slowly darken on the ends.

No alarms went off at dawn
to warn we were engulfed—
no screams of mothers, children,
locked inside the sagging walls,
frantic to get out.

No soldiers—no gasoline.

Just this perfect quiet.
Coffee. The cat.
The *Times* folded back on the table.

Emilio's

Sorry, We're Open!

The young lady is served ribollita
with a fresh chunk of bread and a question:
What is it you prefer about a man—
his propensity to cheat—or to kill?

The young lady is perplexed—first time here—
stares at her soup, steps on her boyfriend's boot,
knocks a can off the counter. *Young lady,*
please don't be upset. We are all friends here.

Whatever you say, please—say it in Greek.
Or Italian. Or even English. Think:
here we are on the brink of disaster
and only you—your answer—can save us.

She thinks. She says, "I don't care for either."
Her boyfriend smiles. She smiles. Emilio
smiles—like Socrates in the Agora:
Ah, good! So then: ta chrimata paidi mou.

My Neighbor

Reality doesn't do it for him,
and he doesn't do it for me: The willed
fantasy. The self-delusion. Fake news
making his day. I say "us." He says "them."
We both say "They live in another world."
But in our worlds we both wear socks and shoes,
we both break bread. I've seen him hug his children.
The last time we argued was over the fence.

Let me say, I was really angry once.
Nobody could come near me. Then this woman—
this gentle, patient woman—took a chance
and laid her hand on my arm. The human
touch. So simple. When I think of it I wince.
When I think of who I was and what one
woman did I look up at my neighbor's house
and shake my head. Let there be peace when he comes out.

To each, to all, to reach the bend
where the path turns again,
and the end, almost in sight.

On the Beach

We are old now,
soon enough—elderly.
But never elders. No.
We are just the old.

The young are everywhere
you look. Younger than
we were when we were young.
Forever young.

The water's shallow,
the sand warm where they run.
The sun beats down
on their brown bodies.

The land feels deep to us,
the water cold.
We keep our bodies white
under umbrellas.

We watch them—the young—
diving into waves.
We gaze out past the reef.
We spy a speck.

We call and point.
The wind blows down the beach.
The sand stings. The waves break.
They do not hear us.

I Like It

for Holly

I like it
when the weather thickens
wetting us with love—

when the mourning doves
nuzzle on the wire
that beads above the road
and the squirrels fidget
on the black bark of the pines.

We knew setting out
that it was about to rain
but left behind our coats, our hats.

We knew that we'd get soaked
and so we have,
and now it's almost dark.

I like your hair like that.

Song: Whatever You Got Going On

Never too late till it's too late,
never too soon till it's done—
never too fast till it's just half past
whatever you got going on.

Never too cold till it's too cold,
never too cool till it's warm—
never too hot till x marks the spot
whatever you got going on.

Today fading, tomorrow waiting, yesterday singing your song.
You got eyes, you can visualize, whatever you got going on.

Never too bad till it's too bad,
never too good till it's gone—
never too much till you're out of touch
whatever you got going on.

Never too light till it's midnight,
never too dark till it's dawn—
never too deep till you're down six feet
whatever you got going on.

Today fading, tomorrow waiting, yesterday singing your song.
You got eyes, you can visualize, whatever you got going on.

Never too late till it's too late,
never too soon till it's done—
never too fast till it's just half past
whatever you got going on.

Bob Gielow

The Culling

Here's a story that asks the question, what is a story, anyway? There is a rich tradition of fictional narratives in unusual formats dating back to the earliest epistolary novels, which present as letters composed by characters all the way to modern stories written as text exchanges. Stories can take the form of legal documents, users' manuals, ad campaigns and lists. "The Culling" deploys the familiar and comforting format of a Wikipedia entry to document a horrific alien invasion. Its clear and calm sentences arranged into orderly and logical paragraphs lull us into putting our outrage to the side, even as we read the twist in the final paragraph. It's been said that science fiction is a literature of ideas, and Bob Gielow deftly unpacks one of the genre's most reliable scenarios. JPK

The Culling

From Wikipedia, the free encyclopedia
See also: Livestock culling

The Culling is the bi-monthly occurrence whereby between 1,000 and 6,000 human beings are rendered mute and unmoving for several minutes, have their bodies float out into an open space, and then move straight up into the atmosphere until they disappear from the sight of others.

First witnessed and reported in March of the year 2015, The Culling was widely agreed to be the Rapture (from Christian theology) whereby a group of people is left behind on earth after another group literally leaves "to meet the Lord in the air." Although many writers and thinkers still utilize theological language and rationales when discussing The Culling, evidence of the arrival and departure of extraterrestrial travelers to Earth timed to coincide with these mass disappearances has led most to conclude that non-Earth inhabitants are taking humans for some unknown purpose.

Origin of the term [edit]

The word culling comes from the Latin *colligere*, which means "to collect". Historically, the term was applied broadly to mean sorting a collection into two groups: one that will be kept and one that will be rejected. The cull is the set of items rejected during the selection process. When done with intent, the culling process was repeated until the selected group was of the proper size and consistency desired. "The Culling" (used capitalized) was coined in early 2016 by Richard Farnsworth, then President of California Institute of Technology, when he and his team of astrophysicists reported to the public that alien space travelers had been visiting Earth twice monthly. Used in this more recent context, it is unclear why some individuals are selected and others are not, and unclear whether the individuals taken or the individuals left behind should be considered the cull.

The phenomenon [edit]

Victims of The Culling experience three known phases, the initial floating stage, the moving stage, and the final departure stage. Mankind does not yet know what happens to the victims of The Culling after the departure stage.

Floating stage

During the floating stage (also referred to as the levitation stage), victims stop breathing and their hearts stop beating. Body position, facial expression and degree of eye openness remain as they were before. Previous activity (i.e., verbalizing or running) ceases immediately. Unless constrained by another object, victim's bodies typically levitate immediately between three and four inches (just under nine centimeters) from their original location. Despite repeated testing, it is unknown to what extent consciousness remains. The floating stage lasts between 16 and 19 seconds. Biometric devices previously attached to victims during this stage indicate no cardiovascular, respiratory, muscular, or digestive system activity. Low level nervous system and endocrine system activity has been recorded (specifically in the Cerebrum, Thalamus, Hypothalamus, and Thyroid Gland), leading many to conclude that victims have not fully died.

Moving stage

During the moving stage, when it occurs, victims' bodies move from their original, levitated location in a direct path to the nearest open space at which the sky is accessible above. While some of the victims' bodies move only inches or feet to get out from under tree branches or a building overhang, others move hundreds of feet to get out of buildings, subway tunnels, or caves. During this stage, bodies have been consistently measured to move at 3.1 miles per hour or 4.55 feet per second (5.0 kilometers per hour or 1.39 meters per second), equivalent to the average speed at which humans walk. This rate of movement does not change when additional weight is added (i.e., when a loved one jumps on their back). Body position, facial expression and eye openness remain constant during the moving stage.

If a victim's body is unable to access an open space because it is in a closed building or vehicle, then it will experience up to six attempts to exit the space. These attempts involve 1) a reorientation of the body such that the feet are pointed in the direction of windows or doors and 2) steadily faster ramming movements into the windows, doors, or walls. Attempts to leave a building or vehicle begin at the same time as most other victims experience the departure stage. While some victims exit the building after one attempt, many (especially during the first several months of The Culling) experience six attempts to leave. Six-attempts victims often suffer significant bodily damage as they are repeatedly forced into windows, doors and walls. Lower bodies and torsos are often crushed during the process.

When the sixth attempt does not lead to atmospheric access, victims remain crushed where they are, though no longer levitated. If a door is not opened during the subsequent Culling, then the body will again experience the floating and moving stages and the six attempts, damaging the body beyond recognition. (It is claimed that Aleksei Yesipov's former body experienced the greatest number of sixth attempts–68–locked in a nuclear power plant outside of Minsk, though his body was no more than cellular pulp when emergency exit doors were opened in 2017.) If a door or window is opened during the subsequent Culling, then the body will move outside and experience the departure stage at the same time as do others. Opening a door or window in between Culling periods will not lead to any change in the movement or positioning of the victim body. Victim bodies can be moved in between Culling incidents, though alteration of the body's integrity (i.e., through cremation) does not alter The Culling activity they will experience at the next full/new moon.

Departure stage

During the departure stage, victims move directly upwards, accelerating to a recorded speed of 213 miles per hour or 312 feet per second (342 kilometers per hour or 95 meters per second). Biometric devices previously attached to victims during this stage continue to indicate no cardiovascular, respiratory, muscular, or digestive system activity. Nervous system and endocrine system activity has been recorded at stronger levels during this stage than was true during the floating stage, though scientists have questioned the reliability of their measuring devices as they travel at high rates of speed several miles up in the atmosphere. Three-dimensional GPS tracking devices, developed soon after the identification of alien space travelers, have indicated that victim bodies travel on a path directly perpendicular to their Earth departure point until they reach the edge of the atmosphere (known as the Karman line—an altitude of 62 miles (100 kilometers) above the Earth's sea level, representing the boundary between the Earth's atmosphere and outer space). Beyond the Karman line, it is believed that victim bodies move straight toward one of eight waiting alien space ships.

In seven known cases, relatives have clung to victim bodies during the departure stage for more than thirty feet. In each case, the relative died due to injuries sustained in their fall back to Earth. During the 24-hour period after The Culling has ended, clothing and items stored in clothing (i.e., wallets and cell phones) have been found falling/drifting back to Earth. Medical devices (i.e., pacemakers) and body cameras from victim bodies have also been found back on Earth.

History [edit]

First Culling

On Thursday, March 5, 2015, at 18:07 GMT, at least 2,934 human beings left Planet Earth in a manner previously unknown and unrecorded. The distribution of this first set of humans mirrored that of the world's population, with the most victims coming from China, India, the United States, Indonesia, and Brazil. Given the simultaneity of the occurrences, losses were documented in the daylight and the nighttime. Lost humans included children as young as four days old (Charlotte Evers) and the elderly as old as 93 (Xiao Lu). All major racial, ethnic, religious and sexual/gender identity groups were represented among those lost. Healthy individuals as well as several terminally ill patients were taken. While two pregnant women were taken with their fetuses, no unborn children were taken from their mothers' bodies. No non-human life forms have been known to be taken. Video images and sound from several dozen episodes were recorded by families, friends, and strangers (i.e., see the documentary The First Culling). By the end of the next week, a list of the names of these individuals was collected and printed by the New York Times, London Telegraph, and China Daily. During early March of 2015, only one reporter (Sven Lundquist from The Copenhagen Post) noted the "coincidence" that The First Culling occurred at the same exact time as the full moon.

Responses to these incidents were described at the time as both horrified and confused. Family members, friends, and neighbors frequently reported their efforts to grab and hold on to victims during both the initial floating stage, the moving stage, and the final departure stage. Multiple reports described individuals whose bodies were thrust through windows and doors, causing damage to buildings and vehicles, before they were swept up into the atmosphere. In several hundred incidents, First Culling (initially referred to as "First Departure") victims could not access the open air from inside planes, cars, and buses after six attempts to break through the physical material/structure impeding them.

The Second Culling occurred on Friday, March 20, at 9:39 GMT and corresponded with both a total solar eclipse and a new moon. At least 5,038 humans left the planet on this date. For a complete list of all Culling dates and times, see The Culling dates.

Reactions to Culling events—2015

By the end of the Third Culling, it was generally understood that Departure Events (as they were originally called) occurred at both the full and new moon. Anticipating the Fourth Culling on April 18th, many people actively planned to avoid leaving Earth by sheltering in a place with limited access to the outdoors. Interior rooms in buildings, buildings without windows (i.e., 33 Thomas Street in Manhattan), bomb shelters, and caves requiring transport via elevators became popular destinations for those hoping to stay behind. As the phenomenon of the six attempts became more widely known and studied, it was generally agreed that having your body repeatedly smashed against walls was not a desirable end-of-Earthly-life occurrence and was heart-breaking for friends and family to witness.

By the end of the Fifth Culling, reliable statistics were being kept regarding the number of victims worldwide. It was estimated that an average of 3,200 people experienced a Departure Event roughly twice per month. Given a world population of over 7 billion, it was estimated that each individual human has a one in 100,000 chance per year of leaving our planet. Compared to the entire world's mortality rate, on average, humans are 100 times more likely to die from other causes than they are due to The Culling. Mortality rates for young (under 40) and healthy humans are similar to the annual rates at which young people were falling victim to The Culling.

In April of 2015, members of the media, social scientists, and many others began to catalogue the qualities and characteristics of those who were lost. Individual names, birthdates, birthplaces, horoscope signs, personality types, illnesses and medical conditions, religious affiliations, racial and ethnic backgrounds, criminal records, the existence of tattoos, "records of sin," and recent activities (including travels, writings, and interactions with others) were all evaluated in some fashion. Numerologists, astrologists, theologians, and even fans of professional sports teams began to make claims that they could characterize those who were departing and/or predict those who would be departing. The World Veterinary Association analyzed the biological and biochemical differences between humans and other animals to assess why other mammals were not departing. These evaluations of who had been lost in an attempt to assess why they were lost intensified significantly when it was learned that extraterrestrial travelers were involved.

In November of 2015, the International Civil Aviation Organization (ICAO) and the US Federal Aviation Administration (FAA) decreed that all commercial air travel would cease twice monthly to correspond with the occurrence of Departure Events and to avoid instances when passengers' bodies were repeatedly being flung against airplane doors or windows (i.e., see Ira Morgenstern). Soon thereafter, calls were made by civic and religious leaders to voluntarily end the use of all motor vehicles for one hour before and after Departure Event times to avoid collisions, property damage, and the additional loss of life.

In December of 2015, social and traditional media outlets reported heavily on "Departure Parties" or "Departure Gatherings" (later called "Culling Parties"). Groups of people large and small gathered to celebrate their camaraderie, shared interests, and their "shared humanity." Doors and windows began being left open to avoid damage from six attempts. Just prior to The Culling time, many people assumed a body position selected as being memorable, dignified, and/or humorous during the Moving Stage (see Jim Carey). While some gatherings offered traditional party activities (i.e., music, dancing, and alcoholic beverages), others included a shared activity (i.e., nature hikes, art-making, or sexual intercourse). Culling Parties have since become a bi-monthly, worldwide tradition for people to spend time with friends and family (in one location or connected digitally), engaged in activities seen as significant, life-defining, and/or worthy of "My Last Act."

Beginning in late 2015, Departure Grief Support Groups (later called "Culling Grief Support Groups") were formed by relatives and friends of victims. Loved ones were/are mourned and remembered in these groups, many of which meet at every full or new moon (depending on when the person was lost). It is common for support group meetings to be offered free meeting spaces, counseling services, memorial messaging (i.e., print, radio, bill board, and television), and food by sympathetic area vendors. These groups often raise funds through Kickstarter and other social media sites for the families most impacted by the loss of breadwinners. A number of bereavement publications and websites have been created focusing on the unique emotional and community needs of victim families/loved ones.

During 2015, Culling/Departure events had little significant effect on international politics or business. While most national leaders openly acknowledged the uncertainty surrounding these events, discussed their concerns, and prayed for the victims and their families, small numbers of other officials 1) disavowed that their citizens were affected (i.e., North Korea), 2) claimed that God had chosen their citizens only (i.e., Pakistan and Indonesia), or 3) argued that their citizens were being victimized by United States and/or Israeli forces (i.e., Iran, Yemen, and Syria). Many regional and national political leaders established support funds (some of them tax-supported) that offered financial support to the immediate families of those who had been lost. Other than bi-monthly closures of international stock markets (beginning December 2015), voluntary bans on travel, and increases in spending on both entertainment (i.e., movies, music concerts, and "high-end dining" prior to full and new moons) and "My Last Act" activities/related-merchandise, international commerce was largely unaffected.

Between March 2015 and January 2016, as over 65,000 total people were being carried bi-monthly into the atmosphere, much of the world's attention focused on the notion of the Rapture. Rapture is a term in Christian eschatology which refers to the "being caught up" discussed in 1 Thessalonians 4:16, when the "dead in Christ" and "we who are alive and remain" will be "caught up in the clouds" to meet "the Lord in the air." For much of 2015, historians, theologians, and many others deepened their studies of (and focused their media stories on) those who originated pre-tribulation rapture theology (the Puritan preachers Increase and Cotton Mather) and those who popularized it (John Nelson Darby, Grant Jeffrey and the Plymouth Brethren in the 1830s and the Scofield Reference Bible in the early 20th century). Theologians bolstered their arguments in support of the rapture with the "evidence" that the six attempts represented 666, the "number of the beast" or the devil. Those who argued that the Christian Rapture was occurring struggled to explain why the leadership of various Protestant denominations (i.e., Anglican Communion, Presbyterian Church, Methodist Council, and Lutheran World Federation), the Pope, and all Catholic Bishops did not "ascend to the heavens." (In fact, during all of 2015, it was reported that only four Christian clergy members, five Rabbis, three Muslim Imams, three Buddhist Monks, and one aide to the Dalai Lama were among those taken worldwide.)

Identifying alien objects

On January 13, 2016, Richard Farnsworth, then President of California Institute of Technology, called a press conference intending to "further mankind's knowledge of the circumstances surrounding the mass human departures" that had been occurring. Joined by a team of eight scientists and six technicians from the Palomar Observatory, Farnsworth provided an overview of the data they had collected since April of 2015 "proving" that "multiple non-Earth-based objects" had been arriving just outside of Earth's atmosphere at times that coincided with both the full and new moons, and with the instances when humans were levitating in the direction of outer space. Although no objects were visible to the scientists, stars and distant galaxies were lost from sight of the Hale and Samuel Oschin Telescopes in a manner indicating that objects were blocking the incoming light. Data collected indicated that at least four of these unknown objects were arriving at "Earth's doorstep" directly above set positions, as if they were in Earth's orbit. The Cal Tech team estimated that these objects became positioned at between 70 and 80 miles from the Earth's surface (between 115 and 130 kilometers) and were positioned there for approximately eighteen minutes.

Data later collected by other observatories around the world indicated that the number of unknown objects was actually eight and that they were positioned at just over 78 miles above the <u>equator's sea level</u>, (126 kilometers—with correspondingly higher or lower altitudes depending on the heights of mountains and the distance from the equator—see <u>Equatorial Bulge</u>.) The size of these objects as they face the Earth is estimated to be approximately 100 feet by 50 feet (30 by 15 meters—roughly the size of a basketball court). It was also learned that the eight objects were not spaced evenly into <u>octants</u>, as first assumed. Instead, as observed by MIT <u>Human Geographer</u> Arnold Spitz, the objects were spaced such that equal numbers of humans lived underneath each of them.

At this first press conference, Farnsworth refused to "venture a guess" whether the light-blocking objects contained or were controlled by "alien beings." He did, however, offer his conclusion that humans were being taken away from Earth by "some force within these objects, as if in some kind of Culling." He offered no explanation for why humans were being taken or what happened to them once they left this planet. He ended his comments by saying, "I'm not sure we will ever understand the reasons behind The Culling." As has been widely commented on by the media and various blogging communities, Richard Farnsworth would later become a victim of The Culling on October 16, 2016.

After the January 2016 recognition that "non-Earth-based objects" were involved in The Culling events, international politics and business were impacted significantly. Over a series of five months, 193 <u>United Nations</u> member states agreed unanimously 1) to convene an ongoing <u>special session</u> and to keep their delegations in <u>New York</u> until the "threat has been averted"—February 2016, 2) to cooperate fully with a "<u>Communications Committee</u>" tasked with messaging the alien beings and attempting to discern their motives (see below)—March 2016, 3) to "apply all available resources" towards the goal of understanding The Culling events (including the biological reactions of victims; the physics of the floating, moving, and departure stages; and further assessments of the qualities and characteristics of those who become victims) —March 2016, and 4) to share both rocket engine and guided weapon systems knowledge, along with launch pads and airspace, to prepare for the possibility that missiles might need to be sent to "attack Earth's invaders"—June 2016.

During the first nine months of 2016, many employers began to implement bi-monthly "Culling time-off" for employees to be with their families. Major cultural and sporting events such as "March Madness" playoff games, Chinese Dragon Boat Festival, and television's Emmy Awards show were rescheduled to avoid full or new moons. Universities avoided scheduling classes and hospitals avoided scheduling surgeries during Culling times. Governmental agencies organized "Buddy Up & Open Up" campaigns encouraging people to not be alone, and to keep doors or windows open and accessible during the twice monthly Culling Timeframes.

Attempts to interact with objects

In February of 2016, NASA, the Russian Federal Space Agency, and the China National Space Administration, supported by the Union of Concerned Scientists, began making both navigational and tasking adjustments to 23 of the 1,100 active satellites orbiting the Earth. Satellites were selected based on their proximity to previously known orbital locations for the unidentified objects and on their ability to collect electromagnetic (or any other signaling) data coming from the objects. Other than confirming that "non-Earth-based objects" were temporarily positioned above the planet, authorities have indicated that "no currently understandable data" have yet been gathered. Without offering any explanation as to a cause, authorities have also reported that five of the satellites used for this purpose have ceased functioning. Some members of the media (i.e., Dana Priest from the Washington Post and Matt Pearce from the Los Angeles Times) have claimed that scientists and leaders have learned more from these satellite studies than has been shared with the public.

After Elizabeth Bleacher wrote a March 2016 editorial promoting the idea in London's The Sunday Times, individuals began purchasing and utilizing body cameras at the full and new moons. On the chance that the body camera owner became a victim of The Culling, the goal was to record both video and sound that would document the event. Loved ones left behind would have a recording of the victim's last moments on Earth and scientists would have additional data they could comb through to better understand the phenomenon. The wearing of body cameras has been credited with the discovery that most victims are quietly humming/moaning during the departure stage. Regrettably, it's been found that some form of electromagnetic interference ends all body camera signals soon after victims end their perpendicular trajectory and as they begin their movement towards alien ships. Body camera debris has been found among victim clothing/belongings that drift back to Earth. In December of 2017, the President of the People's Republic of China declared that all Chinese citizens would be required to wear a body camera twice per month.

In March of 2016, the Federal Communications Commission (FCC) in the United States, the Ministry of Science and Technology (MOST) of the Government of the People's Republic of China, and the Ministry of Communications and Mass Media in Russia, and an additional 78 governments agreed that "every organization broadcasting audio or video content via any electronic mass communication medium must allot "every minute of the three hour time overlapping full and new moons" to a series of Welcome to our planet messages." These messages, in the language of the sending country, attempted to introduce the human race and also describe humanity's "peaceful intent." In the 16 weeks that these messages ran, they became increasingly desperate and hostile, ending in August of 2016 with some version of the following: "Because you have not responded to mankind's repeated attempts to communicate with you, we are left with no choice but to assume that you represent an invading force. We intend to respond accordingly." (See "Final Message.")

In May 2016 through June of 2017, NASA, the Russian Federal Space Agency, and the China National Space Administration combined forces with the commercial firms Virgin Galactic and SpaceX to send a series of probes to the region just below low Earth orbit (LEO) in an attempt to gather more information than had been gathered by existing satellites. These probes were specially designed to gather any and all signals that might be coming into or out of, and to transmit visual images of, the unknown objects, and to transmit them back to Earth in real time. They were also tasked with assessing the direction from which, and speed at which, the objects arrived and departed. Because the unidentified objects locate at an altitude that has proven to be impossible for man-made satellites to establish sustaining orbits (Sputnik orbited at an altitude 55 miles higher), scientists found that locating their probes at the proper altitude was problematic. As occurred with the satellites, the probes (named Culling One through 14) confirmed that "non-Earth-based objects" were temporarily positioned above the planet but did not provide any "currently understandable data" for scientists. Reports that three probes were destroyed "by external forces" (see Miami Herald and Houston Chronicle) have neither been confirmed nor denied by the authorities.

Attempts to destroy objects

In February through July 2017, several attempts were made to destroy the unidentified objects. The Laser Weapon System or LaWS (a directed-energy weapon developed by the United States Navy in 2014) was reportedly deployed first from the USS Ponce (an Austin-class amphibious transport dock) and then from a specially-designed platform at the rear of two different Antonov An-225s. The US Navy and US Air Force reported that in the firings from both the USS Ponce and the An-225, the targets were further away than LaWS was designed to strike and that the power of the beam was weakened by the distance it had to travel. (Note that the An-225 flies at a maximum altitude of 36,000 feet or just under seven miles, leaving it about 70 miles away from the targets.) It is not known if the laser beams directly hit or had any noticeable effect on the objects. Note that there are currently no known operative orbital weapons systems, laser or otherwise, based on a functioning satellite. The United States, China, and Russia each claim to be developing such systems.

According to leaked reports, at least seven attempts have been made to date to destroy the unidentified objects with Tomahawk Missiles, Intercontinental Ballistic Missiles (ICBM), or similar non-nuclear weaponry. Although the United States, British, Israeli, Russian, and Chinese governments are not responding to requests from citizen groups and the media for further information, officials from Lockheed Martin Space Systems and Raytheon have indicated that the directional precision of each of their respective systems was not built anticipating strikes on small objects (roughly 5,000 square feet in area or 450 square meters) located miles outside of Earth's atmosphere. Self-propelled guided missiles were typically built to navigate within the atmosphere and are targeted through use of radiation, radio waves, and/or visual contact, all of which have proved problematic for these targets. ICBMs were built to travel outside the atmosphere, but the accuracy of their strikes was intended to be based on available geophysical information related to the Earth's surface (i.e., GPS) and not to target on air born/space born objects. Some in the media have questioned these claims of "missile incompetence."

To date, no nuclear warheads have been used against the unidentified objects. Political and military leaders, members of the media, and bloggers across multiple nations have engaged in fierce debate regarding both the efficacy of, and the dangers involved in, using nuclear weaponry. Until recently, most arguments against "going nuclear" have included concerns regarding the potential for worldwide radioactive fallout and the fear of retaliatory strikes from aliens. As of late, more and more people have argued against attacking the objects by putting forward what some have called "fatalistic" claims that the alleged alien beings are unstoppable in their pursuit of human victims and/or are taking "sustainable" numbers of victims. Groups such as "Supporting The Culling" compare the 75,000 to 80,000 people who become annual Culling victims to a yearly net world population gain of 70,000,000 and argue that The Culling phenomenon is helping to mitigate this planet's significant over-population challenges. Other groups, such as "Avenge The Victims," have argued that "every possible military option" should be applied in order to "destroy the evil beings who have perpetrated these crimes against our species." (See Victim group vs. supporters debate, below.)

Impact on life attitudes [edit]

It is generally agreed that mankind's perspective towards life has been altered significantly by The Culling. After the collective initial experience of confused, fearful, and angry reactions, the American Psychological Association (APA) and the International Association of Applied Psychology (IAAP) recently reported on studies that fully one-third of Americans and Europeans have both "accepted" the ongoing nature of The Culling and are either supportive or neutral towards its occurrence. After spiking dramatically in 2015 and 2016, instances of panic attacks and a broad category of Culling-related anxiety disorders have reportedly now been decreasing.

Given the continuing uncertainty regarding an explanation for The Culling, human use of protective charms, amulets, and concoctions has become widespread. Many forms of jewelry, clothing, items located around the home, food, drink, and inhaled vapors have been claimed to protect the owner from The Culling. Some so-called "protective" items have been found floating/falling back to Earth (see Mjolnir or Thor's Hammer), thus discrediting their efficacy.

In the three plus years since The Culling first occurred, participation in religious life has increased at the same time that the acknowledgement of secular/humanist world views has increased.

In the United States, for example, social scientists (see Jane Ebel) have documented how the 70% of Americans who had previously described themselves as belonging to or being raised within one specific religious denomination (i.e., Catholicism or Methodism) were more likely to attend church/synagogue/mosque on at least a weekly basis than was the case prior to March 2015. In the same studies, Ebel found that the 30% of Americans who would have previously described themselves as being atheist, agnostic, a religious skeptic, or religiously unaffiliated were more likely to "admit to friends and relatives" their beliefs.

At first, The Culling was not being discussed in most of the world's elementary and middle schools. Educators indicated that they did not want to frighten the children and that they wanted to respect each family's right to present the facts and discuss the theories within the context of their unique values. Now, the National Education Association (NEA) and World Education Research Association (WERA) have each issued statements arguing that young children should be taught about The Culling, that they should not fear it, and that they should "endeavor to live a life rich with knowledge, connections, and experiences" on the chance they may fall victim.

Despite "Supporting The Culling" claims that human losses due to The Culling have mitigated population increases, birthrates have begun to increase within the past year, especially within western societies, due to concerns regarding the potential loss of "only children."

Victims group vs. supporters debate [edit]

Media and Culling bloggers have focused much attention on the debate between Lucy Lawson, Spokesperson for "Avenge The Victims" and Thomas Ortega, spokesperson for "Supporting The Culling." Lucy Lawson is a Pasadena, CA (USA) lawyer who lost her daughter Rebecca to The Culling in April of 2015. Thomas Ortega is a sociologist at The Universidad Nacional Autónoma de México (UNAM—National Autonomous University of Mexico).

Contentious and overtly personal at times, this debate between these two individuals can be summarized by the position statements of each group.

From avengethevictims.com: *"It is with horror that we regularly witness our loved ones being taken. Mankind must fight back to both avoid further loss of life and to avenge the innocent lives that have ended so abruptly. We urge our political and military leaders to use every possible military option to destroy the evil beings who have perpetrated these crimes against our species."*

From supportingtheculling.org/english: *"While the loss of human life that has occurred during The Culling is tragic, it is clear that the alien beings are taking sustainable numbers of victims, are utilizing technologies far advanced to what mankind possesses, and are capable of causing much greater damage than what has already been witnessed. We believe that aggressive military action against the aliens will not prevail and will, instead, create incentives for them to kill more of us or even destroy our planet entirely. We believe that a peaceful human response will be more likely to lead to benevolent alien behavior."*

Ms. Lawson has argued that she would rather see all of humanity die in a battle with the aliens than see them continue to "steal away with victim after victim after victim." Mr. Ortega has maintained that human life has been "shocked but also enhanced" by the steady loss of victims, given that "the threat of random, imminent death has motivated people to live life more fully, seeking stronger connections with each other and aggressively pursuing meaningful and memorable activities."

Views on rationale [edit]

Many scientists, writers, political and religious leaders believe that human bodies are being taken by alien beings to be used in some unknown fashion. Given our inability to communicate with these aliens, it is impossible to understand why this has been occurring. Theories offered have included 1) food for the aliens, 2) test subjects for alien medicines, 3) the harvesting of specific bodily parts (e.g., the Cerebrum, Thalamus, Hypothalamus, and/or Thyroid Gland), 4) bodily incubators for alien babies, 5) an attempt to save the human species from an impending galactic-level disaster (given the rarity of intelligent life), and many other hypotheses.

While the majority of people polled indicate that they do not want to become a victim of The Culling, roughly 12% of survey respondents in the U.S. and European Union indicated their hope that they will "be chosen." Instead of considering them as Culling "victims," these "Chosen Activists" believe that those who leave Earth have been chosen for some "higher" though unknown purpose. Given this perspective, people lost during previous Cullings are revered, studied, and imitated. Instead of using protective charms, amulets, and concoctions to not be selected, these people pursue techniques and make lifestyle decisions that they believe will lead to their being taken.

Many Culling commentators ask questions that are driven by philosophical and spiritual disagreements, uncertainty, and/or a search for an unambiguous "meaning of life." These questions seek to explain how The Culling fits into or alters an individual's or a group's previously held beliefs on the topic. For those who have concentrated their discussions on the individually-focused question of "What is the meaning of *my* life?" The Culling has invigorated attention on personal fulfillment, consciousness, and "doing your own thing." For those who have concentrated on the collective question of "What is the meaning of human life?" (i.e., a "higher meaning"), The Culling has raised many questions on which religious and spiritual leaders have struggled to agree. While Secular Humanist group leaders have reported being emboldened by The Culling, several leaders of traditional religious groups have admitted to "significant struggles" trying to understand and explain The Culling within the framework of their beliefs.

One key element in all Culling rationale discussions is whether people are chosen or whether their "selection" is random or based purely on luck. Social scientists, members of the media, medical statisticians, and many others have offered numerous theories on the human qualities and characteristics that increase the likelihood that someone will become a Culling victim. For every promising quality that is identified, multiple examples of disproving cases are then found. The Gallop Organization (United States), Angus Reid Strategies (Canada), and Allensbach Institute (Germany) have each completed public opinion polls that document significant increases in percentages of respondents who indicate that Culling Selection is random.

Some theorists have likened The Culling to the human breeding, slaughter, and consumption of livestock. In these arguments, as is the case for farmed cattle, hogs, and turkeys, human beings (the "victims") are unaware that their lives, the length of their lives, the circumstances that lead to death for some members of the group, and their actual deaths are dictated by "controlling beings." In many of these discussions, human existence on Earth has been referred to as "free range."

Jane C. Elkin

The Colors of Mourning

In a narrative that stretches from sea to shining sea—from Kittery to Maryland to California—Jane Elkin sails readers through an even vaster swath of emotional terrain. At once humorous and devastating, this snapshot of just one year in the author's life ruminates on the loss of a parent, the return to one's roots after years living elsewhere, and the everyday delights and infinite challenges of updating an eighty-six-year-old cottage perched on the edge of the water. When, amid collecting shards of pottery and sea glass that arrive on her shore and fighting with perplexing plumbing, the writer faces a catastrophic new loss, the reader floats along with her through months of grief, the memoir skillfully weaving between narrative and epistolary formats. Much like the sea glass she collects—forged in tumultuous waters, smashed, and reshaped—Elkin's life has been transformed. In a gift to her readers, she deftly demonstrates that even in anguish, there is beauty to behold and abiding love to sustain us.   MAC

August 2023: George Washington Stept Here

On November 2, 1789, in a nod to Maine's existence under the parent-state of Massachusetts, our nation's first President symbolically set foot in the town of Kittery during his first tour of the thirteen states. This meant crossing the mighty Piscataqua at Portsmouth, New Hampshire, my hometown. It was a distance further by half than his crossing of the Delaware, with the fastest current on the Eastern Seaboard—twice as swift as a seal cruises. The principal ferry landed at Rice's Tavern on the King's Highway to Portland, an inn said to have hosted such dignitaries as Benjamin Franklin.

The jetty remains at the cottage I inherited from my father, a child of immigrants, who lived to ninety on a youthful diet of potatoes, kielbasa, and bread with lard. Could George have envisioned such a turnover when he tarried until the next slack tide? He went cod fishing that day, but twelve hours gave him time for two meals, several rubbers of whist, and a little *jollification,* as they used to say.

Because barmaids back then threw the broken crockery and trash in the water, I also wait for the tides and erosion's gifts of sea glass and china shards. I like to imagine George dining off the fragments that ornament my knick-knack shelf. Considering his stated preference for *a good pipeful of hemp,* perhaps he scranched one of my clay pipe stems between his miserable teeth. It was my daughter Julia, who spent a summer unearthing Pocahontas and Powhatan's village in Virginia, who identified those ceramic fragments.

Discovery is half the fun of a new home, and I plan to fully indulge heading toward retirement with my husband. From the emergence of spring's varied blossoms to the mapping of the sun's rays as they creep through the rooms, my husband Herb and I are eager for secrets beyond the blue willow dishes and green cake set of former tenants. Some things we may never know, like the story behind the secret closet under our bedroom eaves and the hidden radio wires in the attic. Who put them there and why? The smutty novel, copyright 1932, tucked in the basement's false ceiling. Did it belong to the architect who built this place in '38, only to hang himself five years later in the workshop next door, or the judge who lived here after him?

"Never let this place leave the family," Dad urged when he bought it twenty years ago, following my mother's death. His meaty hand on my shoulder and intense gray eyes told me this was more command than request. A lifelong shipyard worker and miser, he saw this property as the culmination of a life's aspirations. "It's too special," he insisted, despite decades of neglect and a regrettable subdivision into an up/down rental with two kitchens. He was inordinately proud of the built-in hutches, carved moldings, sturdy beams, and deep waterfront, all hallmarks of quality and wealth in his generation. Our many contractors concur; they've *never seen such a solid home.*

But oh, the work to be done! At 73, Dad was not quite the handyman he'd been at twenty-two or thirty when he bought his first two fixer-uppers. After an initial attempt at sprucing things up, he let the place decay around his La-Z-Boy. Now we are deep into discovering the extent of that decay. The furnace looks crusty, like it may not survive winter for lack of bandages. The pipes are a mish-mash of spliced copper and lead. The kitchens and baths, not just dated but gross. Is that knob-and-tube wiring? How many coats of reglazing on this patchwork tub?! Is there asbestos in those walls? Lead in the peeling paint chips as large as Fritos? Herb needs to know. In his bureaucrat's eyes, we own a Superfund site.

Three doors down, someone has leveled a sweet old cottage to build a modern monstrosity of sharp edges and glass piled high to block the neighbors' views of the river. We couldn't afford to rebuild even if we wanted to, which we don't. So now, with so many big issues needing attention, I scrub, reupholster, and rearrange the existing furnishings, rather than purchase new ones. Julia, with her artist's eye and athlete's frame, scavenges a mid-century modern record cabinet from a bedroom and jockeys it downstairs next to a similar-style bench in the sunroom, where she likes to sketch. We remove several schooner paintings from the crowded walls, and Dad's squall of nautical kitsch is magically calmed. The room looks almost balanced, despite the 3½ foot model man-o-war on the bookcase and harpoon over the door header. I'm all for tossing them, but she insists they stay in his honor. She loved her PopPop and all his quirks.

The yellowed shades with their brittle handles and furred edges must be my age, but after trimming yards off each roll to expose the pristine cores, they don't look half bad. I wander the rooms, cleaning rag in hand, pondering how many microns of dust it took to transform white sills to gray. How many years of tarnish on the antique nickel fixtures I mistook for blackened bronze?

None of these things, however, matter half so much as questions of the future. How much longer can the garage's cracked foundation keep it from sliding into the sea? How long can the locust trees and lilacs hold the embankment when just last week there was a historic 13-foot tide nibbling at their roots? Julia, a sea level rise specialist, looked skeptical, chewing a lock of her long brown hair as she considered the situation. How long until we run out of money turning this disaster into a dream home?

Thank God for thrift shops and the dump's Freebie Barn, where I find an antique nightstand, picture frames, and a driftwood plaque proclaiming, *It's all gonna be fine.* It's a message that bears repeating as we head into kitchen and bath renovations with the first frost.

Herb ascribes to Murphy's Law, but I live by Yhprum's Law: *Anything that can go right will go right.* Optimism is what I bring to this partnership, and the law of averages is on my side. After forty-five years away, I realize that I desperately want this place—not just any house near this place but this particular house that my widowed dad was so ill-equipped to make into a home.

The Piscataqua is my home, first and last. I was born eight miles from this spot in a town named for its harbor. I grew up across the river in a neighborhood named for another harbor. As a Navy spouse, I called five bodies of water home, from Puget Sound to Lake Neuchâtel in Switzerland, to the Chesapeake Bay; but the Piscataqua remains the one where I feel "at home."

My mother used to joke that I was the only girl who had to leave Portsmouth to marry a naval officer—as if that were my goal, which for her, I believe it was. Her control was the primary reason I left and stayed away. But this is where I belong: where I awaken to the gulls' cry and fog horns, where the rocky beaches are strewn with mussels and kelp, where summer nights are chill and winter snow is dependable but fleeting, and where there's always haddock at the seafood market.

In my mind, it's already Memorial Day with the lilacs in full bloom as we enjoy the first lobsters of summer with family. Yes, Dad, it would be nice to pass this place on to the next generation. Maybe Julia will follow through on her dream of relocating from California. She has always loved it here, and now at thirty-six and still single despite being the most beautiful woman in any room, she's losing patience with Mr. Maybe. It takes a certain kind of man to think he stands a chance with a woman like that, and they don't seem inclined to commitment. A New Englander by birth, this is where Julia feels her roots after a lifetime of visiting, and a local job has come up that is just suited to her talents.

If not her, maybe her sister's family near us in Maryland. Alice is approaching burnout as a night-shift nurse with three children. We used to joke that she was going to save all the babies while Julia saved the world. She is strong on tradition, instilling a love of this seacoast in Mason and Natalie, who make sea glass and shell art with the booty we find together, while little Nolan is bent on throwing every pebble from the jetty into the river. This street already bears their surname, a name I see all over town, though my son-in-law knows of no connection. It would make Dad proud for his family to progress from immigrants to founding fathers in four generations. And why not? It's a free country.

February 2024: Perspective

Herb worries about the mushrooming scope of construction and its progress, or lack thereof. We're a month behind schedule for want of a plumber as one after another gets sick. The third, echoing the previous two, refuses the job unless we replace all the pipes.

Having just been promoted to his dream job after a decade of waiting for the boss to retire, Herb wants to be there on-site to supervise the work but can't spare the time. So, we make the ten-hour drive to camp out for a weekend so we can assess the project. There's no going back now with the three most essential rooms gutted, so I heat water for a sponge bath in Julia's college hotpot and cook breakfast in her dorm microwave. The water meter from the supply main juts two inches from the foundation, prompting new concerns about its viability. What if it breaks and we must excavate—in winter?! This is how my husband's mind works. *It's all gonna be fine,* I say, hoping I am right.

Two weeks later, on the eve of the replumbing job, we're binge-watching *Ozark* when we get a call from some hospital with a Berkeley area code. Julia is in the ICU with a brain bleed after being hit by a car.

That can't be right, I think. I just talked to her last night, and she was fine. Best she's sounded in weeks, since the breakup with her boyfriend.

It can't be too serious, I tell myself; she had the presence of mind to have someone call.

Should we cancel life to go to her?

Of course.

But going means accepting that she might not be OK, and that cannot be. She is beautiful and vibrant. Tragedies happen to other people.

Then it hits me, no one else knows. She is all alone in some hospital bed, clinging to life.

I call her friend Becca, the one contact she gave me in case of emergency. It's a number I never seriously thought I would need.

Fifteen hours later, we are waiting to board a plane when the contractor calls, and suddenly his concerns feel trivial.

It's all gonna be fine, I reassure Herb vaguely. I pray I am right.

March 2024: On Our Own

One month later, we head back to Maryland with half of Julia's worldly belongings packed into her Subaru with the *I brake for wildflowers* bumper sticker. She was such a minimalist, I found it both baffling and admirable. But *there are many different ways of being human,* as she used to say. It's a motto I am working to remember. *WWJD* is another. *What would Julia do,* I often ask myself toward that goal of being one with humankind.

Something about tragedy brings out a oneness with others. Two days after the accident, feeling grateful for Becca's efficient care and optimism about Julia's progress, I went to the hospital coffee shop and noticed a young Black man come in wearing a muscle shirt and gold chains. He was unusually soft-spoken for such a big guy, and I had to ask him to repeat himself before I understood he wanted napkins. When I motioned to the dispenser on the wall, he moved there trancelike, buried his face in the cheap paper, and heaved several silent sobs. In that moment, I felt inexplicably drawn to this stranger with whom I'd formerly have thought I had nothing in common. When I asked if he needed a hug, he crumbled into the arms of this gray-haired white lady. "This is the best hospital in the county," I reassured him, confident that the doctors had already saved my daughter as he shared pictures of the car wreck that put his brother in the ICU. I hope he made it. Julia, I learn within the week, will not. It was Ash Wednesday, I later realize. I gave up my daughter for Lent.

On that bleak day, I left her bedside a moment for the lobby bathroom and found two dozen of her friends and coworkers lining the hall like an honor guard, all eyes glued on me. Her friend Andrea, who reminds me most of myself, stepped forward with a brown paper bag. "*I have a gift for you from Julia,*" she said. Inside was a sweater she made in high school: charcoal gray with skulls emblazoned on the sleeves, and as warm as a hug. Miraculously, it fit.

Young women compliment *Skully* wherever I go, and I tell them my daughter made it.

Then a waitress asks if she can buy one, and I feel compelled to tell her why that is not possible.

I don't do it for sympathy. I just want the world to know how proud I am.

On our way home, listening to her road trip playlist of Tom Waits, Zack Brown Band, Bob Dylan, and the like, we notice signs of her presence all around us, rainbows in particular: in sunny California, in the foggy Grand Canyon, and directly overhead in a clear blue sky near home. Heart-shaped rocks and cacti sprout up in our path like lucky pennies through Joshua Tree, Desert Hot Springs, and The Petrified Forest. Have there always been so many, or are we just more attuned to them now? The desert sun sinks behind a hoodoo, and I don Skully just in time to drive around a curve and see signs for *Skull Rock*. Julia would know how to milk this photo-op for something special, but I'm not her and I'm just glad to be smiling.

Stopping in the New Mexican wilderness at night, we admire the Milky Way, as clear as a textbook photograph. As I stand in the open sunroof, bare arms bathed in a soft breeze as I drink in the grandeur and silence, I wait for the hoot of an owl. Julia told me long ago that if she were an animal, it would be an owl. Owls wink, and she only had one good eye. They are calm and wise, like her. Surely owls are hunting at this hour, but there are no hoots, no dramatic silhouettes in the headlights.

I think a lot during our journey about the overused phrase *senseless tragedy*, as if any tragedy makes sense. It makes no sense that she was hit in a crosswalk on a steep hill just days after writing in her journal that she was grateful to Berkeley's terrain for keeping her fit. It makes no sense that she had a massive brain swell just hours after the ICU doctors discharged her to a step-down unit with the words, *She's probably out of the woods.* It makes no sense that she of all people was taken so young when she was doing so much good in the world while others are bent on destroying it. She just saved a thousand-acre oceanfront ranch in Sonoma County from development, and that was after only three months into a new job. What else might she have accomplished, given the chance?

I have read that anger is a normal and expected part of grief, but I don't feel it. If we're all here for a purpose, I figure she just accomplished hers earlier than most. But why am I not yet allowed to join her? What have I neglected to do in sixty-four years beyond raise a family, teach hundreds of children and immigrants a new language, and use the singing voice God gave me to praise him? When can it be my turn?

Two weeks after our return, Andrea has a strange story to relate. Something about a medium she's known for decades, a Bayou Catholic named Shanda, whom she consulted about work. *A friend recently died,* Andrea warned, *but if she were to arrive, I'd want to know.* Sure enough, at the end of their business, Shanda says, *Julia is here. She had a terrible head injury. And what's this about a jacket she's showing me?* Shanda has our attention. Andrea kept the jacket Julia wore on that fateful day. *Julia says that she wants you to know she is free and happy, and that she is always with you.* She goes on to give advice to her friend and ends by saying, *I have a message for my mother. She'll know what it means. Tell her I'm sorry. I thought I knew everything, but no one does. We're all here to learn.* Oh Julia, please don't apologize. I have a thimbleful of regrets where our relationship is concerned.

April 2024: Always with Me

Dear Julia,

Nine hundred photos! That's how many I have of you on my phone. Your friends are so generous, and I've gotten quite adept at taking pictures of pictures for your memorial slide show. My neighbor Amy is putting it together because, as you so eloquently put it, I am a Luddite. The video is twenty minutes: five songs, starting with You Belong Among the Wildflowers *and ending with the comic relief of a jet zooming around the globe to* The Happy Wanderer. *I hope you love it. I haven't worked so hard on a project since my master's thesis six years ago, when you surprised me by traveling all the way from California to Vermont for gradu-ation. Thanks again for being there.*

Two months I've waited for your owl, but still it eludes me. I read in a book about signs from the other side that if I want a specific sign, I should issue the request precisely and verbally.

So, here it is. I want an owl TODAY, so I'll know you're here. Thanks in advance.

Love, Mom

That day, I encounter the word *owlet* on a list of baby animals for my ESL students, and I miss the connection. I see a Delft owl in a department store two hours later, and still don't get the message. Then I go to a garden party at the historic home where I give tours and notice for the first time a huge owl atop the neighboring mansion. At last, there can be no doubt! I watch and wait for him to fly off, ruffle his feathers, or swivel his head, but he just sits there like a decoy. Damn. Fooled again. Then I remember, the book said to keep an open mind; spirits are not literal. Wow, three in one day. How many have I missed, wanting what I want instead of what is right in front of me? Isn't that just like life?

Herb and I drive north to check on the house, specifically the new emergency generator hook-up, and we hit such traffic that it's after midnight by the time we roll in, road-weary and oddly wired. We flip on a light, and it immediately winks out along with the security cameras and all the nightlights. *What did he do?!* Herb exclaims. Just then, the generator kicks in, and he charges to the basement yelling for me to *stay there!* I hear the metallic creak of the breaker panel door and my first directive, *Open the fridge and tell me if the light is on.* We check every room as he frantically maps out our new buffer of coverage. As it turns out, a car crash knocked out power to half the town, allowing us the perfect opportunity to address our main concern.

The next day, he tackles the monumental task of relocating Dad's treasured garden statue, *Mabel,* about whom Julia wrote a highly amusing essay. A midget-sized strumpet with my mother's Rubenesque figure, Mabel has leered from the place of honor in the backyard for fifteen years, hiking up her dress to the garter belt while her bosom fairly spills from the boa around her enormous rack. It's not easy moving her downhill to the beach, given the bumpy ride each time she rolls onto her bust, but finally she has her toes in the sand where she can summon the passing cargo ships. Lasciviously licking her lips, she appears to call out, *Hey Sailor!* And I think this is where she belonged all along.

On my way to the coffee shop our final morning, I note a detail on a house I've passed a dozen times before without seeing it: a door knocker like a winking owl. Good morning, Julia.

June 2024: Retreat

I came seeking peace
bearing pieces of you
to smooth out my grief's edges:
your charcoals and urn, your photos and sketches
in each room, on every shelf
help me reclaim bits of myself

Dear Julia,

Did you realize what an old-school homemaker this house belonged to before PopPop's grime and grease took hold? The built-in ironing board in the kitchen shows the wear of decades, but the seamstress in me is rabid to save it. It reminds me of the one my mom pilfered from the attic of the junior high where she taught Home Ec. There's a bottle of curtain-white by the slate set-tub in the basement, a product I never heard of. Under the kitchen sink are both silver polish and Brasso for the light fixtures and trim plates behind the crystal doorknobs.

You would not believe, or maybe you would, just how gray the mattress protectors had become. It must have been obvious a year ago when we took ownership, but inconsequential compared to more dire health hazards. Remember the brown oil slick staining the underside of the kitchen cabinets from PopPop's deep fryer? The carpet of crumbs under the recliner and TV cabinet that we swept clean at each visit? The half-eaten chocolate bars in every room just begging the vermin to chew their way inside? Did he not care that it took a month to eradicate the Norway rats from under his neighbor's porch?

The renovated kitchen is a step back in time to an era when white meant sanitary and basketweave tilework was the tasteful choice. How fortunate that both are back in style. The antique cupboards with their snowball knobs look quaint. The new fridge, tall and narrow enough to fit the niche formerly occupied by the broken range, saves us ten steps across the kitchen and around his old dinette. The matching gas stove in our new cooking peninsula feels positively commodious, despite being a compact. *You warned me not to go with an apartment sized stove, but you were wrong. I could almost cook Thanksgiving dinner in this thing. Maybe some year I'll try.*

Best of all, I love the scalloped wood valance framing the double window. It reminds me of Rhea Perlman's kitchen in the Barbie movie. Remember that hilarious Barbie photo shoot you did with the exotic costumes Mom knit when I was little—the Victorian in the parlor bowing at the piano and nipping from the sherry decanter; the apron-clad Hungarian herding my miniature carved geese; the Spanish dancer doing a high kick; the blonde in gold lamé and Sixties updo asking her child to Get yo' momma another mimosa, Bobby Sue. *Ha-ha. Oh, and that sweet close-up of one doll's hand fastening the bridal buttons on another's gown.*

Sometimes I worry I'm going to forget you, and then I think, who could forget Robin Williams, Lauren Bacall, or Rachel Carson? You are all that and more.

Love, Mom

Unfortunately, Herb couldn't join me for the whole summer, which I finagled off work. Nevertheless, he encouraged me to come north and will visit when he can. So, I cooked a freezer's worth of meals before I left. Determined to get back in touch with my creative side, I've brought my journal and laptop, my neglected ukulele, a new calligraphy set, Julia's art supplies, and her thumb piano. Only the latter holds my attention for the first month. That, and napping. I'm like a leaky helium balloon floating aimlessly from room to room, playing games on my phone, turning a few pages of fiction, and baking for the neighbors while streaming audiobooks on the afterlife one after another after another. Each time I use the rubber scraper, I am reminded of toddler Julia licking the batter and taking entire bites out of the aged rubber—then asking for more.

My creative energy goes toward turning this house into a home. Like my beloved Aunt Marguerite who found joy in crisp linens and a swept sidewalk, I clean the final layer of construction dust from the furniture and find that the treasures just keep coming. Tucked behind a curtain is a set of photo-coasters Alice gave my father in 2010: images of her and her husband taken during their first trip north to meet her PopPop. They look so young and carefree.

I hang a photo in my bedroom of Julia running across a mountain ridge at sunset, a gift from a friend I haven't seen since high school. She lifted the image from Facebook, where Alice posted about her sister-the-organ-donor who saved six lives, recounting how Julia sewed skirts from Basmati rice bags and dresses from tablecloths, and concluding that *she's been preparing her whole life for this.*

Poor Alice has it hardest of all, I fear. After growing up as close as twins and being separated by life's obligations, she arrived at her sister's bedside too late for conversation. She became the night watch instead, monitoring her medical condition until it was time to grant her permission to cross over. I blame myself for telling her Julia would be more alert once she got to rehab. Now she carries that memory plus the knowledge that she will someday bear the burden of our care alone.

Another friend, perhaps with Julia's affinity for plants in mind, sent a lush peace lily. I don't have her way with greenery, but *Lily* will be the exception! I put her on a windowsill with dappled sunlight from our massive maple. She thrives until the first thunderstorm blows her off to face-plant on the floor. I try a sheltered corner of the yard where I can see her from the Adirondack chairs where I spend my days under the tree's canopy, one of the original reasons I saw myself summering here. Back home, Maryland's punishing heat and sun exacerbate my autoimmune illness, limiting me to a crepuscular existence. This shade tree, like the reflective parasol Julia gave me, buys me some freedom.

I slather on some SPF 100 for a jaunt to the grocery store and am approached by a young woman who tells me she hasn't eaten in two days. She is clean, well-mannered, and riding a nice bike. Whatever circumstances put her in this predicament, I don't want to add to her disappointments, but I was raised not to give cash to beggars for fear of how they'll spend it. Quashing the urge to check my purse for small bills, but eager to get out of the sun, I pause to suggest several charities that serve free meals. *That's all right,* she says politely. I'm pulling out of the parking lot when it hits me, WWJD? I should have taken her to Panera, just as Julia used to take homeless women to CVS, even when she could barely make ends meet for herself.

Maybe that's why she's in Heaven and I'm still here.

Because our waterfront is entirely shaded in the morning, I begin my days beachcombing for sea glass. The variety is astounding: multi shades of white, beer-brown and green, violet, aqua, blue, and red, some tumbled but mostly clear and jagged. There are squares and triangles, asymmetrical shards, and perfect diamonds, emeralds, rubies and citrines, ready for mounting in a ring such as I'd hoped Julia would wear one day on her ring finger. Sorting them is Zen therapy.

The 24th rolls around and, oblivious of the date, my biological clock tells me it's been another month since she died. But what was the actual date? Though her death certificate says the

25th, we all sensed her spirit checking out before that. *What was the real date, Julia,* I ask aloud. *Show me a sign.* Within the hour, she does exactly that as I stroll past the laundromat and see a huge sign proclaiming *OPEN 24 HOURS.* I text Shanda to share this news.

Shanda resolved all my questions and then some back in March during a two-hour phone call for which she didn't even know the sum of the check I'd put in the mail. Our interview included an appearance by my parents, complete with their ailments and Boston accents, in which my mother expressed her love and apologized for driving me away. Then came her rationalization that *she didn't want me to be the free spirit she'd been, and that I was a little stubb'n* (stubborn). And here I'd thought death brought enlightenment! I was laughing and crying, and then came Julia's final statement about the reason she remained single. *The reason I didn't get married,* she said, *was because I didn't want to be controlled, and I only attracted controlling men.* "So, you see," Shanda concluded, "you were a success as a mother because you gave her the freedom you were denied."

Shanda texts me daily ever since, prayers and positive affirmations mostly. In return, I send her images of the sea glass fish I'm now obsessed with making, and a watercolor of the house Julia did two years ago. Now she responds with a courtesy phone call for which she wants no money and ends up talking for an hour about all she sees in Julia's picture of the house and the land. *Who's the man in uniform,* she asks, and I say I don't know; an inn stood on this property for two hundred years. *Did someone die there?* Possibly. *Did a woman give birth there?* Probably. *Does this house have a plumbing problem?!* she exclaims. *Not anymore,* I reply.

Julia always makes her presence known in one way or another for my houseguests. Walking along a sandy beach with the widow of an old friend, we see two red-winged blackbirds swoop past to peck in the sand like plovers. We decide it's our departed loved ones. Though those birds inhabit the nearby marshes, I've only ever seen gray ones along the shore. The owner of my childhood home invites me and another friend in for a tour, and there in the foyer is a stained-glass owl in the window. Didn't Julia say, *I am always with you?*

July 2024: Independence Day

Dear Julia,

I'm making progress on homemaking, but my standards have risen with the renovations. New linens today, floor shopping yesterday, dinettes last week. Meanwhile, your favorite space, the sunroom—or half of it anyway—is now yours. Flanking the bench under the window where you liked to work, by the interior wall, is your two-tiered Fifties end-table and that lamp with the mirror-shard base, and your plant stand is on the other side overlooking the water with your urn on it. Well, it's not exactly overlooking, as it's too short and snugged in the corner, but I trust you can see. I've polished and strewn abalone and other shells from your favorite beaches all around it so you will feel at home. Yes, I know you're dead and can't feel anything, but I feel your presence, and that will have to do.

Love, Mom

We gather for a memorial picnic with Alice's family and my few cousins who remain in the area. One, who lost her only child a year before we lost Julia, is still in the depths of grief. At seventy-five, and with nothing to fill the void, she may never pull out.

After the meal and before fireworks we will watch from the backyard, the sun sets to the strains of jazz floating across the river from Prescott Park, and we gather in the sunroom for a brief memorial. I'm in the midst of the eulogy when little Nolan tiptoes in to tell Alice and Herb that *there's a beaver in the backyard!* They charge out to save the food from what we fear is a nutria we've been monitoring for months on the critter cam, but he's already gone. When we ask for a description, Nolan launches into a pantomime that includes a flat nose and whiskers he calls *long cheeks.* Then in a second recitation for the camera, it has a long and pointy nose with sunken cheeks and sharp claws. If I ask him a month from now, it may have fangs. Such is the nature of memory for most.

I have a talent for remembering. I remember my bedroom when I was two, before my father fixed the cracks in the wall that looked like a witch in the evening shadows and morphed into a lily by morning's light. I remember what Herb and I both wore and entire snatches of conversations from our courtship forty-three years ago. I remember picking Julia up from her nap at two months old and feeling her snug into the crook of my neck and pat my back as I always patted hers. I remember heeding that little voice in my head that said I should spend that critical night in the step-down hospital with her on her way to rehab, how she reveled in the Mexican hot chocolate I brought her after a week of Ensure, and how she kept asking if I wouldn't be more comfortable in her bed. Then I remember her blank stare when she fell into a coma counting to one hundred as I clutched her in my arms and begged her to stay. I only wish I could forget. Or do I? I was with her when she came into this world and when she left, and that is a privilege I need to honor.

I had planned to bring her urn back home for the winter, but that seems wrong now. She never loved Maryland the way she did Maine. She was content on her own, even gallivanting around the world. She deserves to rest in peace, and I need to find peace without her.

Four months, I have tortured myself with *What ifs*. What if she hadn't gone running that day? What if she'd taken a different route? Better yet, what if she hadn't relocated three months before? What if the driver weren't an unlicensed 85-year-old? What if she hadn't fallen out of bed onto her head during that first night in the hospital? What if her HMO hadn't been so quick to transfer her to a smaller hospital without even a neurologist on staff or an ambulance available when she needed an emergency craniotomy? What if she'd woken up and gone to rehab as planned? Or woken up but was never the same?

This is where the questions stop so the healing can start. The past is unchangeable and the future unknowable, so I will live in the *now*. I will embody her best qualities to keep her memory alive. This will not be the summer I imagined, helping her heal, but there's a boatload of healing happening, nevertheless. I may not be productive, but at least I don't cry all the time.

August 2024: Progress

Dear Julia,

Happy Birthday. This year, instead of sending you gifts, your friends sent each other gifts that remind us of you. My favorite is your version of Georges Barbier's Art Deco painting L'Oiseau Volage. I know you didn't intend it for framing, but I love it. You had the best friends.

I'm planning to paint a floor cloth for the foyer. It will be so much cheaper and easier to clean than a carpet, but I wish you were here to help. I printed and framed a poster in the style of Edward Hopper, one of your favorite artists as I recall, showing a beautiful young woman in red wistfully gazing out to sea from a beachside café. She looks so much like you, I did a double-take when I saw it. There's a globe light hanging starkly against the blue sky, which I mistook for the moon. I didn't know how devoted you were to the moon until I kept hearing it from Shanda and your friends. Becca tells me that whenever you went camping under a full moon, you put your rings out in a bowl of water to recharge. I'm not sure what that means, but it makes me smile. It fits. How did I not know this about you?

You certainly had a lot of rings, half of them my cast-offs. In your baggie of personal effects that the hospital gave me was my silver and citrine ring that you wore for a decade. Whatever power it had, personal protection, it appears, was not one of them. More likely, the power was creativity. You were such an extraordinary artist, really coming into your own with your minutely detailed drawings of flora and fauna.

I've displayed your artwork and photos everywhere, including the tasteful nature nudes you devised of yourself with starfish and scallop shells. They used to make me laugh, but now they just make me smile, as if I'm merely passing you each morning at the bathroom threshold.

Love, Mom

September 2024: Saying Goodbye

Dear Julia,

Something remarkable has happened. My pen is flowing again, not just in random calligraphy images of my closed eyes' imaginings, but in poems and prose. After seven months of writing paralysis, it feels like a rebirth. My mind is working again, too. The puzzle I couldn't frame two months ago is flying together as I see color and shape connections that eluded me. Maybe it's the two recent Supermoons. You said, via Shanda, to watch out for them in order to connect with you. I guess it's working. Yesterday, a stranger complimented me on Skully, and I told her you made it—without going into detail. I don't need to burden others with my tragedy.

It's time to put this house to bed for the winter and head home. Dad and I will pack up the porch and foyer in preparation for Round Two of renovations before hitting up the Deerfield Fair tomorrow and driving south on Sunday. I miss Alice and the kiddoes, my students and friends. I look forward to the migrating waterfowl and maybe doing a musical this winter. I do not look forward to seeing your empty bedroom, though, with the new curtains I made right before your accident. It's hard to believe you won't ever see them or sleep there again.

You already know, of course, but I was ecstatic to see that your teenaged kidney recipient I follow on Facebook went elk hunting for the first time in his entire invalid life and bagged a huge stag with one lucky shot. I know you had a hand in it, my little one-eyed Annie Oakley with the astounding aim. He looks so happy in the photos, as I know you are.

I think I might be happy again, too, if I didn't have to go. I cried this morning like I haven't in months. But it's time. I'm needed there. But unlike George Washington, I'll be back . . . again and again and again.

Love, Mom

Straightening up to leave, I stow a teapot on the top shelf of the china cupboard and spy one last treasure I'd tucked away the previous year before it had meaning for me. It's a small vase of sea glass—not just any sea glass but the hazy variety in shades of white, sky blue, and cobalt—the hopeful colors of mourning.

Paul Goodwin

The Long Perspective

Like the best light verse, Paul Goodwin's poems display a shiny veneer of wit and verbal play while allowing an undercurrent of wisdom to emerge—a testament to his lifetime of careful observation and reflection. Though the poems gathered here confront aging, mortality, and loss, they do so unblinkingly, head on, and with wry detachment. Throughout, Goodwin's honed images flash with startling insights, because he knows the best poets must always pack a metaphoric switchblade in their jeans. RF

Alexandria

The instant she died,
A cloud of history
Sighed from the house and
Drifted down the street
Like mist off a lake,
Disappearing in the evening light.

Scrapbooks sagged,
Their meaning vanishing

As aunts and grandparents
And decades of friends
And occasions diminished.
Names and stories evanesced
As the photographs flattened
Into forgotten strangers.

Keepsakes dulled,
Lost their narratives.
Their roots shriveled in the deep loam
Of sentiment.
One second they were rich reminders,
The next just trinkets.

When an old person dies,
It's like a library burning
And she was Alexandria
And now as lost as that legend
Of charred pages, parchments
Lore, learning, love.

Consolation

No matter what you say:

Now he is with god,
It was quick,
It was a blessing,
She didn't suffer,
He was so brave,
Our prayers are with you,
Here's a casserole we made,
You still have the children,
Everybody loved him,
What a way to go!
Terrible . . . terrible,
Only the good die young,
I'm so sorry for your loss,
Of the deaths of all my friends, his hurts the most,
When the history of mankind is written, this name
Will stand as a beacon of humanity and heroism,
Or (emperors only),
Now he is a god.

Still dead.

Cowboy Poem

We've all lost friends and stood around
That squared-off six-foot hole in the ground
And tried to think of something nice to say
To take the sting out of a shitty day,
Then stumped to a saloon for a drunken wake
And cried some tears for our old friend's sake
And you told some yarns 'bout what he meant to you,
A few of which may even be true.

Unless you're built unsentimentally tough
And see clear-eyed through scary stuff,
You probably got as the wake wore on
A vision of yourself as dead and gone
And wondered what your friends might say
To honor you on your burying day
And what would happen if you were the last
With no drinks raised to you after you'd passed.

So if you work on your health every single day,
Watch what you eat (so it doesn't get away),
Keep an eye peeled for what wants to eat you
And exercise and be wise in everything you do,
You just might win the headstone prize,
Live a little longer than the rest of the guys,
But don't fool yourself or ride too high
Because good health is just the slowest way to die.

Cowboys and cowgirls wherever you are,
It's tough to be alone with your belly to the bar.
If you outlast your kin, your friends, your wife,
That means you're living out a lonely life.
Everybody knows how the story ends,
But I'd say don't pray to outlive your friends.

My Education in Print

I have avoided,
By a clever program of delay,
Having my earlier, inferior work in print,
Waiting calmly for the day
When my now-mature style
And store of hard-won wisdom
Will flow perfected from my pen.

Or, more likely, I will just expire,
Packing my uncollected works into the void.
Posterity, were it aware,
I'm sure would be annoyed.

Little Poem

Little poem
In the middle of the page,
Surrounded by white blankness
As far as you can see,
With no explainer,
No excuse maker,
No one to tell about your
Conception, your difficult birth,
The changes you've gone through,
What of you has been erased,
What hoped for,
Worked on,
Worried about,
Celebrated,
Lost.

You're standing now
On your own feet.

I know how you feel.

One Year After the Mast (2019)

After they are folded, the thousand cranes stop being a spiritual challenge and become a storage problem.

Nobody knows for sure
What tells the woods
To stage a mast year
With acorns and beech nuts
Raining in abundance.

But the nut-eaters notice.
The harvest fuels a flurry of rodenty lust.
And, come spring,
The gray squirrel population explodes.

But the trees, having dispensed their bounty,
Do not repeat the feast.
And the yearlings,
Stomachs empty and brains full
Of no wisdom and no experience,
Widen their foraging worlds,
Braving the roads
Where New England's top predators roam.

Any ten-mile stretch of highway
Is now thick with victims
Felted flat, with the occasional tail
Blowing free or tiny paw
Pointing to the sky,
But mostly just abandoned gray slippers
With fading red trim.

It's as if nature, having folded
Her thousand squirrels,
Is pleased to have help
Refolding the excess flat again.

Refinement

There is a moment
In the life of a white cotton T-shirt
When the wear and washings
Have scrubbed away the last vestiges
Of lint. And all that's left is
Thin as silk
And slides over the body
Like warm wind,
Weightless,
Perfected at last
Before it rips and frays away
To the rag bag.

And we, plain cotton that we are,
If our luck holds, may find
Our aged selves abraded to a purer state,
Clearer, sheerer, stripped to what's been
Holding us together all along.

Should I Be Worried?

It's a good question to ask your doctor
Hoping for reassurance,
Your partner, after a minor tiff,
Your boss with a wry chuckle
That fools no one,
Yourself, when your brain won't let you sleep.

Sometimes it's obvious.
The endless seconds it takes to answer your phone
At 4:00 in the morning
Are an excellent time to worry.
Likewise, when the HR person asks,
"Can I see you in the conference room?"
Or when anyone at all says,
"We need to talk."

But sometimes it's not obvious at all.
When you feel winded
After a flight of stairs,
Or a second friend younger than you
Dies,
Or a parent tells the same story
Twice in one phone call,
Or you get a registered letter
From the IRS.

Of all the stupid advice ever given,
"Don't worry" is among the stupidest,
Right up there with "Cheer up!" or
"Don't take it so hard."
You do or you don't.

They say worry kills.
But they don't say

What kills worry,
Which is a hardy perennial.

Pop Sonnet

We take our music with us as we age
And keep the gods who made it in our hearts
As one transforms into a tuneful sage
While others die or simply fall apart.

Bob Dylan, Joni Mitchell, and The Boss
Still speak to us as they did in their prime.
Their voices sing of hope and love and loss,
The rocks and rapids in the stream of time.

These artists must be watching us as well.
And see their fans are turning fat and gray.
Our shrinking numbers have a tale to tell:
Depleting ranks who knew them in the day.

From youth to fame to passing from the scene,
Our music shows what generations mean.

Rolling

If there comes an hour when everything seems right to you,
Family, friends, lovers, leaders, the world,
You may hear people complain
But you won't know what they're talking about.
If you are aware, take pictures, make memories, diarize relentlessly.

Pay attention.
The years will leach
Every element
Of that perfection.
All veins of gold come to rock.

And one day
You will look back,
Astonished, that your perfect world
Is gone, gone, bloody gone.

It's hard to avoid
An occasional "When I was young . . ."
But with each "In my day . . ."
You admit to the world
(If not to yourself)
That your day has passed.
The young are carving Thanksgiving
In the other room,
And you don't know what they're talking about.

Bad Tenants:

I blame the earth.
It should have killed us long ago.
It's tried, I know,
But ice ages, volcanoes,
Even plagues
And weather (what a laugh!)
Up to and including droughts,
Never brought the breeding population
Down enough.

And now, the infestation
Is getting really serious.

I hate to blame the victim
But the earth has known for eons
That we were not good tenants,
Would crowd out other residents
Killing whatever could be eaten,
Or sewn into clothing or hung on a wall,
Cutting down what could be burned or built with,
Turning oceans into garbage dumps
And tearing down mountains
To get to gold or iron or coal.

Even for humans,
Getting rid of bad tenants
Is a hard slog.
But the earth
Is no doubt thinking
In geologic terms.
The occasional mass extinction
Creates room for promotions,
And you can't say the ants
Haven't put in their time.

I'll be gone before the seas
Break over the wall into Manhattan
Or the next avenging asteroid thunders down.
But it would be fun to see
How our ruins compare to the Greeks or Aztecs
When the aliens answer the ad for settlers
For a newly vacated planet.

No Longer In Service

At some point
The failure of a friend
To be in the accustomed place
Or return the call
Is no longer trivial.

We need a button to push
That will send the message,
"I'm all right, thanks"
To our web of friends,
A begonia on the balcony
That signals health and persistence.

And, of course, another
That sends,
"I'm sorry. I've gone
And won't be back,
Ever,
It was good."

Single use.

In case of emergency,
Break heart.

Insulation

The trouble with having
An open mind,
Is that people will try
To put things in it.
Revelations just don't stop
Even if you want them to.
And every new piece that you add
To your Amazing Human Brain! kit
Changes everything.

Whatever your life seems
To you: gauntlet, race, battle,
Stroll in the garden,
Zombie death march of teenage angst,
Or guest spot on someone else's
Talk show,
If you want to continue
Being who you are
(Or who someone says you should be),
You must be ever alert
To keep your brain unprofaned,
Your mind-shelves cleared of alien thoughts.

Safeguarding ignorance
And armoring dogmas
Is a full-time job.

You learn something every day
If you're not careful.

I Was Warned

My youthful 32-inch waist
I surrendered bite by bite.
I knew better, of course.
I decided early on
That I can't eat
All I can eat.
But snacking is one sin
You can commit three times a day
Year after year.

My aching feet are down to
Decades of hard footwear.
The feet tried to negotiate with the shoes
But leather, used to keeping
An entire cow inside,
Wouldn't listen.
(And I thought the shoes looked great.)

For hearing loss, I blame
Speakers as big as station wagons,
Headphones that let me
Blast Stratocaster anarchy
Without bothering my neighbors.
The wreckage of my hair cells
Can be chalked up to
Black Dog Satisfaction.

My brown-blotched skin I sacrificed
On the altar of the sun.
I loved the lying out, but always knew,
From seeing the spotted
Hides of my elders,
That damage was being done.

My other casualties—eyesight, hair,
Digestion, creaky joints,
Spotty memory, waning optimism and more—
I regard as design faults,
And take no responsibility for.

Mixed Media

Poetry dying?
What else is new?
Poetry is always dying.
Drama has been dying for three-thousand years
And poetry was ancient
When the first actors trod the Grecian dirt.

Fiction's doin' pretty good, ya know.
Can't complain. Covers the earth.
Something for everyone,
Highbrow to much lower on the body
And sequels always on the way.

Talk is healthy as a horse,
On the surface,
But it's a symbiote,
And its companion animal, Listen,
Is supine, hooked to a monitor.

And yet the barque Poetry,
Holed at the waterline,
Canvas a-tatter,
Sails on, outside the commercial shipping lanes
With its weighty freight in small packages,
No use to anyone, until it is,
And then just what the doctor, the lover,
The mourner or the thoughtful need,
Whether they ordered it or not.

Lost

I lost my mother
Before I found myself
And lost the time we should have had
For her to tell her story
And me to hear.

It took me too long
To realize how hard the vanishing
Of that precious tale
Would bite.
It's the great, lost novel
I can never read,
The unrecorded campfire tale
Told while I slept.

She lost her mother at two,
Grew up with a disappointed father
Who chewed tobacco and hid
Pint bottles behind radios,
And stepsisters who always got a little more sunlight.

The telling might have done her good:
And now, 46 years after
Her death
At the hands of several rounds
Of bad luck,
I know it would me.

Her loss hurts
As much as ever,
But maybe less often.

More than any other name
On my lengthening list of deaths,

Regret about hers comes in waves,
And aches like an unset bone.

At My Age

At my age,
I know what you mean
When you say
"At your age . . ."

It means you have found fault
With my demeanor, weight, language,
Attire, grooming, politics, taste
In music, tolerance of children,
Or stubborn insistence on
Continuing to be who I have been
For seven decades.

You mean that I should eat better,
Drive faster, update my electronics,
Embrace new music, recycle more
And generally act more like someone your age.

But at my age
I know enough to invoke
The age-old formula of the old-aged:
Wait 'til you get to be my age
And then apologize to my hovering spirit
For your total incomprehension
Of what it means to be
My age.

And, in the meantime,
Fuck off.

That Daydream Again

The high-powered poetry agent,
Hoping to align our interests
And make my success his success,
Asks if I'm willing
To tour
In support of my blockbuster
Chapbook.

And what would it take, he asks,
To get me off the Hoot circuit
And into the top poetry venues
Like Robert Frost Stadium
Or the Bard Bowl,
Or even private readings
For billionaires' birthdays?

You've outgrown the trophies
And thousand-dollar checks, kid,
He says, time to make up your mind.
The poetry Big Leagues are there
If you want them.

There's gold in them thar stanzas,
And if you're ready to take your shot,
You're just one Fresh Air spot away from
Good Bones territory and Oprah.
Hell, if things break our way, I see
A presidential inaugural gig,
A chapbook musical on Broadway.
Even, just two words, kid,
Super Bowl halftime!

You've got the chops,
And there's big money in Big Poetry,

He says, but it takes a Big Poet!
Say the word and I'll book the readings.
And when I hesitate, he adds,
You're not getting any younger,
You know.

Because

If my father had not truly
Loved my mother,
If he had not hugged her
When he came home from work
Like a man given a glass
Of water in the desert,
If he had not stayed with her
Through her illness
And wept at her funeral,
Then I might not believe
In true love.

But he did.

So I do.

Bus Terminal

As the bus pulls in,
She is on the platform,
Bouncing softly
On the balls of her feet,
Smiling the half smile
That will ripen into a grin
When the anticipated hug
Happens.

On the seat in front of me,
He does not bounce,
But I sense the
Unseen, parallel smile
Warming his face.

He has come home
To her.
And she is home
To him.

And that is all I know of them,
Two people at a bus station
Happy for their reunion.

But it is enough,
However long it lasts,
To make me glad for them,
And to remind me
Of what I miss.

The Early Winter Thing

Maybe there is no wood to haul,
Split and chop for kindling,
No fires to lay,
Light, tend, feed and poke,
No ash to shovel, coals to dig out and revive
In the pale, stinging dawn.

Maybe there are not sweaters to knit,
Socks to darn, nets to mend,
Decoys to carve, ice on the pond to saw,
No cows or horses to pull food down for
Nor buckets of steaming milk to lug inside.

The first reaction, when the air sharpens its knife,
Is to turn inward—browse, scroll, text, binge, DoorDash.
But huddling around our devices is not enough.
There is still winter work to do.
Simply enduring is not enough.

We must arm ourselves, gird for a siege.
Tune the skis and skates, fill the feeders,
Relearn the painful joy of blood inching back
Into hands and feet.
Sing loud, sing long.
Gather at the groaning board
With people who know how to eat and drink
And laugh.

Darkness and cold are on the earth
And cold and darkness work on our souls,
Turning the screws of shorter, darker days,
Until, to our amazement, the axis of the year appears
And Solstice signals the annual pivot from dark
To light and lighter still.

There will be plenty of time for depression and fatigue
In the depths of January and the solitary confinement
Of February, when all the chocolate in the world
Will be only a temporary balm.
But we can endure anything
If we know it will end.
Get up!

Bang!

Like us, the universe
Had a beginning,
And may,
Like us,
Have an end.

The details of our individual beginnings
While clear in theory,
Violate the historic taboo
Against imagining our moms and dads
As lusty beings
And our personal genesis
In a parental Big Bang.

The origin stories of the world we inhabit—
Every culture has at least one—
Offer a rich smorgasbord
Of explanations, many involving
Preexisting gods
Doing the generative nasty.

As for the universe,
Which has been expanding for billions—
And grown as our eyes opened—
For hundreds of years,
It's either religion or physics.
Either the preexisting Big Something
Snapped its fingers,
Or the preexisting Big Nothing
Burped.

Do you prefer your nothing
Plain?
Or with personality?

My favorite origin story
Comes from a cosmologist
With a poet's soul, who
Put the origin of everything
Down to "an imperfect nothing."

That's a mic drop line
If I've ever heard one.

Active Shooter Alert

Like it or not,
A collective decision has been made
By just enough people to matter
That it is a reasonable response to rage—
Or disappointment
Or impotence
Or a sense that the world has gone fracturingly wrong—
To kill one's self
And take as many people with you as possible.

This act—suicide with an attendant court of victims—
Has its own rituals,
Its own language,
Its own aesthetics,
Its own way of keeping score.
"They may not cry for me," it says,
"but they *will* cry."

And we survive each day
Knowing that, soon, more lives
Will swell some depressive's last act
Into a significance
That his life never had.

In a world where the only coin is fame,
There are no innocent victims,
Just collateral damage among the guests
As shooters consummate their marriage to
Whatever despair or angry god moves them.
And it doesn't take many who believe this
To twist cracks in the world's foundation.

Advice

Pack for the climate, dress for the weather.
Always put $2 on the gray horse.
Cheap, comfortable, stylish—only two to a customer.
Shoes are the only wardrobe item worth overpaying for.
Facts for the meal, truth for a condiment.
It seldom hurts to ask.
Call your mom.
Even a sound boat needs a bucket.
Write it down.
Don't do that (you know what I'm talking about).
Get over it.
Know how to find your light.
Don't take it personally.
Be stubborn, but pick your spots.
Don't be humble, you're not that great (Thanks, Golda).
If you never fall down, you're not going fast enough.
Your best decisions come, not from your heart or head,
but from right behind your belly button.
Keep a lime in the kitchen, just in case.
Keep your knife sharp.
Don't give advice.

Attitude #3: Letting Myself Go

I have been thinking
About letting myself go.
The question is,
How far?

Start with a pair of baggy-at-the-ass
Khaki pants topped
With a sweatshirt revealing
My food choices for the week.

Shaving? No.
(And when I do, I'll leave
Triangles of missed stubble
Under my jowls).

I'll dial back my flow of babbling wit to grunts,
Supplemented by monosyllables,
Or two at most,
Muttered under unpleasant breath.

I'll get my news from newspapers
Scrounged from coffeeshop tables,
Lay in cans of Dinty Moore beef stew
And corned beef hash
To supplement the boxed donuts
And instant coffee that
Will get me through the day.

I'll draw the line at drinking.
Alcohol turns a principled
Rejection of style and conformity
Into a greasy stairway to hell.

This isn't about you; it's me.
It's a finger flipped at my own
Desire to be respectable, reliable, safe.
After a life of caring what other people think,
It's a temptation.

At root, it's not that I don't care,
It's that I don't want to care.

Is this a good idea?
Please advise.

Suspicion

My body and I have been a thing
For a long time,
And we've gone everywhere together.
But no matter how well, or
How faithfully it has served me,
I expect it, at some point,
To be unfaithful,
To betray me.

Like a jealous lover,
The longer we go
Without this happening,
The surer I become
That it will.

I have no idea
How or when this might happen.
But I suspect it may
Split us up
For good.

After all we've been through,
It will be a shame
For it to end
That way.

The Guy's Recipe for Guacamole

Halve and scoop the two fugitive avocados
That were hiding behind the
Orange juice.
Chop too much onion
Too coarsely using the wrong knife.
Add the juice of one
Hard-as-a-rock lime that
Still smells okay.
Mush together and sprinkle with salt,
Then more salt.
Optional: briefly consider adding
Tomatoes (don't have any fresh
And don't know if the five-year-old bag
Of sun-dried is still edible).
Could also add garlic,
But am already on the couch with a bag
Of corn chips and a beer, so . . .
Too late!
Serves four, unless you're alone,
Then serves one.
Enjoy!

New Hampshire Idée Fixe

Once you have conceived the idea
That a man, coshed by his wife's boyfriend
In the parking lot of a New Hampshire mall
During a snowstorm late on Christmas Eve,
A propitiatory pair of expensive earrings in his pocket,
His body scraped into the growing mound
Of snow by the plow driver too drunk to notice,
Not to be found until the crows are seen
Pecking at his hand as the ice pile melts in April,
Once all that's in your head
It's hard to pass the mall in spring without
Looking for the crows.

Madeline Kearin

Witch Hole Pond

What's wrong with Molly? We ask this continually as we read "Witch Hole Pond." Clearly she is unhappy, but her estrangement from the life she has made for herself is more complex than garden variety melancholy. What draws us to her character is the lushness of her perceptions of the natural world as she and her husband wind along the trail around Witch Hole Pond. He has the right of her problem: she is an overachiever in "catastrophizing," imagining the worst possible outcome of every twist of fate. Because of this she is searching for a kind of safety that involves withdrawal from the world. What will she do when she catches a glimpse of a possible "tidy, circumscribed, solitary life" in the magical (or is it imaginary?) house she discovers on the far shore the pond? Hers is a story of questions, although some may never be answered. JPK

The trail carved into the woods at an angle, so that after walking just a few yards their view of the house with its armor of moss-matted shingles and fieldstone walls was cut off. As they continued, the trail behind them ducked out of sight. The path ahead rolled up beneath their feet as though it had not yet existed before they came upon it. The forest was coming into being as they paced onward, thrummed into existence by the rhythm of their footsteps.

"I think I left the stove on," she said, stopping suddenly, and the revolving track of the path shuddered to a standstill at the edge of her shoes.

"You didn't leave the stove on," he said. "I checked."

"If I left the stove on, and the cat gets into it, the kitchen could catch on fire and the whole place could burn down by the time we get back."

He shuffled backward from the spot where he had stopped, a few yards ahead of her, and pawed beseechingly at her arm.

"The stove is off. You're catastrophizing."

She didn't move or respond to his touch. When he released her arm, she let it drop like a dead thing. "What's catastrophizing?"

"It's kind of like pessimism for overachievers. Come on."

She paused for a moment before following him, reflecting on the familiar expression that his face had assumed when he realized why she was stopping. It was the same expression he wore as he watched her coming back to bed after getting up for the third time in one night, and when she woke up in the morning feeling like there was a mouse inside her chest. It was the expression she had observed that night they had driven back to the city from his sister's wedding in Maine. He had reached over to take her hand and told her that she was the woman he'd like to marry. She had dipped her head between her knees and retched.

Now his face had returned to its accustomed arrangement, a steadily measured compound of calm and playfulness, and the sun, incising the forest through the leaves, cast a living patchwork of light and dark over his features. He looked like a man that anyone would like to marry. Though he seemed light and cheerful, she knew that there was a spring coiled tightly in him, braced between his wiry shoulders, that was ready to leap into action if he sensed that they were in danger. He had that kind of protective animal instinct, inherited from grandfathers in war and great-grandfathers at sea, that was typically atrophied in a man of their generation, but in him it was vigorous and well developed. Like hers, his mind was a machine engaged in the endless processing of potentialities, whirring through every possible outcome. But while his way of managing the machine was to fortify his defenses in preparation for the inevitable catastrophe, she found herself caught and mangled inside its gears, forced to cycle through its chambers over and over again.

She watched his face as it was continuously destroyed and recreated in the patterns of sun and shadow, and trained her eye on him with a detached, anthropological interest. He was saying something about the vegetables they would plant in the garden in the fall and the fences they would build to keep out raccoons and deer, but she registered the content of his words only superficially. Her attention was attuned to other things, coded messages embedded in the inflections of his voice and in the gestures of his hands, that might make him legible to her in the ways that she wanted him to be legible. What parts of me, she wondered, will you come to resent—or more realistically, resent already? And when you bury those resentments, as you must, in order to keep this thing between us going, will you bury them beneath an appreciation for my better qualities? Or will you smother them beneath the knowledge that you've made your choice—that you are an honorable man who made a commitment, for whom there is only one way forward?

Her distracted brain dully assimilated the fact that the path had begun to slope downward, bringing them into a cooler and darker part of the forest. The ground was softening beneath their feet, the air thickening, while the path ahead continued to meander and twist in a way that made it impossible to see more than a few yards ahead. She thought they had lost sight of the trail markers, and her heart jogged in her throat. But a few moments later they came to a weathered wooden sign, shaped into an arrow that pointed down a detour off the trail, carved with the words *Witch Hole Pond*.

◆ ◆ ◆

Let's leave, she thought, as they turned down the detour and the ground beneath them sank even lower, quickening their steps toward unforeseen depths. *Let's turn around and go back to the house and stay there,* she thought, as the woods on either side of them drew closer as though hurtling toward a far-off vanishing point, drawing them onward with a steady magnetic lure.

She didn't say it aloud, of course, because she had already expended her self-imposed quota of complaints in verbalizing her anxieties about the stove. By carefully selecting the worries she exposed and dispensing them on a regular schedule, she could cultivate the illusion that they were only shallow concerns—not existential crises that wore down to the bone—and that they were relatively rare, fleeting things, rather than a ceaseless interior drone. She followed him down the detour because that was something he seemed to want to do; it didn't matter how much it mattered to him or what *she* wanted. *You give more weight to his thoughtless whims than you do to your own deep-seated convictions,* she told herself. *You'd cut off your own flesh to feed him if he was slightly hungry.* For a moment the raw, pulsing mental image was sufficient to distract her from her racing heartbeat.

The trail felt as though it was staged—it was *performative,* as someone in one of her college anthropology classes might have said, manipulating the landscape and their bodies inside of it in order to render a particular kind of experience. They couldn't see the pond, but they could sense its increasing proximity in the moist air and the deadening of sound and the smell, musty with the earthy notes of wet things left to rot. There was an earnestness and an honesty to the scent of decay that she appreciated more now that she was older—now that the ritualized incantation of anti-aging spells had become audible to her. She found all the talk of staving off age to be disturbing; old people talked about their own bodies as if dealing with things that were already dead, stripped and dehydrated and molded into an uncanny facsimile of life. She imagined living inside a taxidermy shell of herself, the cold clinical measures directed at her desiccated flesh, the sour antiseptic stench of concoctions meant to hold the cells in stasis . . .

You don't need to think about this now, she thought. *You're young and you still have many years ahead of you.* There were no stigmata of age on her face yet (she checked daily). Her body was lithe and vigorous. *Can't you feel your heart working, now, your young, healthy heart, pulsing fresh life through your body?* And its telomeres steadily shortening with every moment, she thought, the chronometers in her molecules winding down like rickety clocks.

Perhaps it was the path, working its tricks, or maybe it was her own distracted mind that effected the illusion, but when the pond finally appeared it was as though it emerged from behind a curtain, as though it hadn't yet existed before they came to it—as though their coming to it had summoned it into being.

◆ ◆ ◆

She wouldn't have called it a pond. To her it was a small lake, banded by a dense circlet of fir trees, its jeweled waters studded with rocks—the type of sand-colored, craggy boulders that proliferated in that part of Maine and were used as raw material for every structure imaginable, including their own little house and the walls around the garden. She would have called it a lake, and given it a different, less spooky name, but what did she know? She had grown up in a suburb, where a pond was what they designated the part of the backyard that grew a giant puddle when it rained, and the stand of five trees along the picket fence was a jungle.

The path led them along the circumference of the pond, and as they walked, the forest changed. At times it was open, allowing a clear view of the water and the trees on the opposite bank, and of the bushy green undergrowth that grew between them. At other times their view into the pond was obstructed by the bleached stalks of dead trees, tilted and braced against each other to form a triangular window through which they could glimpse the insects prickling the surface of the water.

They came to a small bridge, crossing a crooked stream that fed into the pond. The shadows from the trees were particularly close in that spot, as though converging on a central point, a vortex of pure darkness where the air was completely still and bracingly cold. This was where he chose to take her hand. She sensed the warmth of it, the familiar nip of his calluses against her skin, but she was too unsettled to appreciate the gesture.

"Let's go back," she said, against her better judgment.

"Why?"

Because I'm afraid. Isn't that the reason for everything I do? Because on the inside I'm just a panicked animal running through a maze. Where most people have desires and motivation, I have fear. Fear is my substitute for a soul.

She shook her head, unable to answer.

"We're already more than halfway around," he said. "If we just keep going it will go faster than if we double back."

She didn't quite grasp his logic—how did he know that the path went in a loop? But she acquiesced, wordlessly capitulating and resenting him slightly for it as though he were a tyrant who wielded absolute control over her. This was how she passively disenfranchised herself, displacing her own inner tyrannies onto him. She resented him for the suggestions he made, which she accepted unquestioningly, and for the annoying tics and habits— his frozen feet needling her in bed—that she tolerated silently. She had *volunteered* to leave the city, to realize his dreams of building a homestead in the woods, rendering a sacrifice he had never asked her to make and infuriatingly did not seem grateful for. And now they were deep in the wilderness and would likely soon be dead, if not from the malevolent forces she sensed pulsing through that part of the forest, then from starvation when their meager harvest failed to take root.

She was thinking about the garden and of the tiny bead-sized leaves that had only just begun to unfurl along the fine channels in the earth, when she realized that her hand was empty. The trail in its serpentine course had bucked again and thrown him off of it entirely.

◆   ◆   ◆

There was a game she liked to play in her head ever since she was a child. It was called *Escape Hatch.* She had invented it in first grade one morning when her stomach was queasy and her heart felt like a tiny motor purring in her chest. She imagined raising her hand and asking to use the bathroom. The teacher would nod his permission. Then, on her way down the hall, she would turn the other way and sneak out the front door. No one would see her because she was still short enough to duck her head and avoid the gaze of the receptionist over her desk. Once she was outside, she knew the way to get home. She had memorized the route; it was about four miles, only six turns, right-right-left-right-left-right.

Knowing that she could leave at any time and manage her way home on her own accord loosened the tight cords in her gut. The irony of *Escape Hatch* was that in perfecting her plan, mentally mapping its coordinates and choreographing its gestures, the impulse to run away diminished. She never left school.

As she grew up, the game evolved. In her mind, she packed her suitcase and walked three miles to catch the last train home on the first day of college. Before her first date—with a narrow-faced, greasy-haired boy from her art history class named Josh—she visited the restaurant a day in advance and took note of where the exits were and how easy it would be to slip out without his detection. During the first week she worked at the Aldrich Historical Museum she made a habit of arriving early in order to look up the route back to her house on her computer. Of course she knew the route—she had just walked it, after all—but she found it soothing to look at, a visual representation of her ability to flee. If she had to, she could pull the lever on her job—on her life, on anything—and disappear.

At times the game was a soothing and even enjoyable diversion, a way of reminding herself of her own resourcefulness—she wasn't trapped, after all; she was in control, and knowing that she could go or stay, according to her own will, was a source of power.

But at other times the game was a source of humiliation, a revolting habit that she couldn't stop. It was embarrassing to recall how she had opened her eyes just a sliver during her first kiss with the man who was to be her husband in order to make sure that the door to his apartment was still there. If necessary, she was to grab her purse—it was on the hook by the door—and run the six blocks to the bus station. And it was shameful to find, among all of her pleasant recollections of the day, a memory that stuck out from the rest like a shard of glass: that as she walked down the aisle, even as she said *I do,* she had been playing the game. In her head she planned how she would return all of the gifts with a note of apology to each giver. She would ask her Aunt Emma for the name of her divorce lawyer. She would move back in with her parents and let him keep the apartment, but she would take the cat and the Windsor chairs she had inherited from her grandmother.

Thus from the very beginning—sealed into its foundation— there was a cowardice in her role as a wife that went beyond the simple fear of displeasing him (which was in itself a source of significant shame for her, a self-identified feminist). It was a fear of taking responsibility for her own life, her own decisions. Without wanting or asking for it, he shouldered that burden for her. And so, when things went wrong—when he hated his dull office job, when their apartment was burglarized, when they both became weary and disenchanted with the city and the life that he had chosen—there was no one to blame but him. Perhaps that was why he had thrown himself so enthusiastically—almost fanatically—into this quest for a new life, so radically different from the one they had been living.

And now, alone on the edge of Witch Hole Pond, she could comfort herself with the fact that she had done nothing to bring this on herself—or perhaps more accurately, that she had brought this on herself by doing nothing, by being no one but the shallow reflection of a man's desires.

◆   ◆   ◆

She called his name, softly at first, as though to avoid waking something that she sensed lying dormant in the long reeds that shaded either side of the path, then louder, with as much volume as her lungs could muster. She thought of retracing their steps back to the main trail and following it back to the homestead, but what would she do there, in an empty house, while he was somewhere out here, searching for her? The knowledge—as concrete and real to her as any solid object—that he would never stop looking until he found her weighed on her heart like lead. She decided to go onward, to see if the trail looped around as he'd suggested.

The branches of the trees above her slotted together like laced fingers, admitting only small, mobile pinpricks of light onto the forest floor. She was surprisingly calm. His absence freed her from the scrutiny of his gaze. She had spent so much time as a performer beneath the glare of that spotlight that she had forgotten the person she was when it was turned off.

The scene came to her like something from outside of time, like a fragment of a dream that had broken off and fallen into reality. It was a little ramshackle hut made of dark wood and sandy stone. Like a cross between a log cabin and the Pilgrim cottages at Plymouth, it was old-fashioned but belonged to no particular time period: a child's primitive drawing of a house rendered life-size in bristly thatch and unpainted clapboards. It was set into an alcove of the forest with just a few feet separating it on each side from the rutted trunks. The windows, narrow slits without panes, were lit with a ruddy orange glow. There was no motion or sound from the house or its surroundings except the narrow plume of smoke uncoiling from the chimney.

Her husband had once defended them both from a mugger on their way home from a restaurant in the city, throwing the man back with the flat part of his forearm just as he was brandishing the knife. But for all his courage in the face of worldly dangers he had an intense aversion toward any suggestion of the supernatural, ghostly or witchy things, dark tales and horror stories. He had walked out of a theater once during a Halloween showing of *The Haunting* and adamantly refused to listen to her read aloud a passage of Lovecraft. The little house was not overtly threatening like a robber or a murderer; it simply sat there, its very presence a sinister provocation. She knew that he would be tugging at her arm by this point, pleading with her to keep going.

But he wasn't there, and she wasn't bound to his wishes. She walked through the open door.

◆　◆　◆

There was another game she played, less compulsive and more relaxing than *Escape Hatch.* It was more like a daydream or a satisfying puzzle, the kind that required just enough effort to be interesting.

In this game she imagined what her life would be like if she hadn't met her husband, or one of the other men she had dated, or anyone at all. Instead of moving to the city, she would have stayed in Aldrich, working at the museum in the town where she had grown up. After a few years living with her parents, she would have saved enough money to buy a place of her own. Real estate in Aldrich was cheap, and she might have bought a one-bedroom house on a tree-lined street, the kind of house she always referred to in her mind as a Spinster's Cottage. In her cottage every object would be carefully chosen and arranged. She would line up rows of antique bottles on the bookshelves and hang her grandfather's watercolors on every wall. She would have three or four cats and cultivate a reputation as an eccentric. The neighborhood children would know her as the lady who let them pick raspberries from her garden, and she would nurture a relationship with them akin to a distant aunt or cousin, fondly regarded but never intruded upon. Perhaps she would have affairs: discreet, informal liaisons with men who knew better than to ask for her affections or her allegiance. Or maybe not.

She wouldn't wake up to cold feet or hairy legs or have to chip dried shaving cream and stubble from the sink. She wouldn't have to visit his friends or his family or pretend to be interested in the things that interested him. That chunk of her time, of her attention, of her body that she had deeded to him would be returned to her, and her life would be wholly hers. A tidy, circumscribed, solitary life.

The thought of this game came to her as she stepped into the house and surveyed the carefully swept floorboards, the massive timbers bracing the roof, and the cavernous fireplace shuddering with flames. Along one wall, there was a long wooden shelf that held a pewter cup, a pewter plate, and a ceramic bowl. The only furniture in the house—which was all one room—was a small circular table, a chair, and a bed, with high posts and neatly gathered curtains. Baskets and bunches of dried herbs hung from the rafters, forming a dreamy upside-down forest around her head, a thicket of pleasant scents.

Clearly a homesteader, and a much stauncher disciple than they, lived here—some latter-day Thoreau, Helen or Scott Nearing. It was a niche with occupancy for only one, and only one with a hardheaded, spartan type of will, paired with a well-developed receptivity to the humblest variety of pleasures.

She sensed the magnetic pull again, the same weighted sensation she had felt when they had started down the trail, driving her to stay—stay, and enjoy the warmth of the fire and the play of its orange light on the bare wooden surfaces, stay and sink into the bed and wait for new light to blanch the windows, stay and see what shape the days would take inside these warm, close dimensions, molded only by her own hands, by her own wants.

Would he miss me? she wondered. Once the violence and the urgency of grief had faded away, and the passages of life reopened to him, would she prove to be replaceable?

The house performed its spell, sending warm draughts of air from the hearth to cradle her, buoying her back and forth as if rocking her to sleep. But there was another force at work, and she was surprised to find it stronger, more urgent and visceral than she had expected. She took one last lingering gaze around the room and went out.

❖ ❖ ❖

He was right; the trail did circle all the way around. When she came to the end she found him, appearing seemingly from out of nowhere beside the sign for *Witch Hole Pond*. He stepped forward and the structure of his body collapsed around her like a fallen tower.

"Molly. Thank God. I thought I'd lost you."

She dug her fingertips into his back with an animal possessiveness. She marveled at how good he smelled, like leather and earth and wood smoke. Apparently being immersed in that scent all day long, day after day, had rendered her insensitive to it. Their brief separation had lifted her olfactory anesthesia.

"Did you see the cottage?" she asked.

He nodded. "I thought of you right away. I thought, only Molly would appreciate such a weird old thing. It must have been there for two hundred years. I was amazed the chimney was still standing, with the rest of it all in ruins."

She shook her head. "The cottage I saw wasn't ruined. It was perfectly maintained, with a fire going and everything."

He gave her a wry, slanted look, his trademark gesture of skepticism. "We must not have seen the same cottage. This was a wreck with the walls caved in and the roof gone, and trees growing out from the inside. There was a black stain over everything, like it had been burned a long time ago. The chimney was charred too, but it was still upright. And there were some broken things on the ground. Here, I brought a piece for you. I thought you might know what it was."

He handed her a small, hardened nub, the size of her thumb. Whatever it was had burned so hot that it vitrified, turning it into a glossy, iridescent lump, over which five or six different colors crawled at once. She turned it over in her hand.

"Pottery maybe. Or metal. It's hard to tell."

He shrugged. "The whole place spooked me out. I don't think I'll go down there again."

"I'll go back sometime by myself and look."

"You will?"

She might as well have told him she was planning to climb Mount Everest. His eyebrows arched, then settled with the rest of his face into a look of quiet admiration.

She did go back the next day, in the morning when the sun was high and filtered freely through the leaves, illuminating the forest in broad, golden strokes. She found the ruin as he had described, shrugged narrowly into a pocket of the woods along the pond loop trail, a pile of blackened splinters guarded by the crooked chimney, its silent stone sentinel. She went back many times over the next few weeks and months, sometimes bringing his walking stick with her to poke through the rubble, uncovering more of the same brittle, scintillating fragments—none of them remotely identifiable. She always found the ruin, making note of its place about halfway around the pond loop. But no matter how earnestly she searched, she never again found the other cottage, the one with the thatch roof and beckoning fire.

Call For Entries

We seek chapter-length entries of 20-30 manuscript pages for our 2028 anthology (forthcoming fall, 2027). A chapter entry can be an excerpt from a novel or biography, a stand-alone work such as an essay or short story, or a group of shorter works such as a collection of poems, flash fiction, or short essays. Please make sure your entry has at least 15 manuscript pages, and no more than 30. Entries can be nonfiction, fiction, poetry, a mix, or anything in between. Only one entry per author please.

Eligibility

1. Writers must be the sole owner of the copyrighted work submitted. Do not submit an entry with more than one named author. Previously published material will be considered if you retain all publishing rights, and provide a cite crediting the original publisher.

2. Writers must also reside in one of the towns in Maine or New Hampshire touched and drained by the Piscataqua watershed (see map at *https://prepestuaries.org/01/wp-content/uploads/2013/02/2012_Watershed_Poster.pdf*)

Deadline

Entries must be submitted by midnight **Wednesday, September 30th, 2026**, for publication a year later in the fall of 2027.

Entry Guidelines

Send your entry in an email to: *editor@tenpiscataqua.com*. Please include the following in the body of your email:

1. Please introduce yourself in 100–150 words, including something about your writing experience, education, published works, and personal or writing interests, as well as your connection to the Piscataqua watershed. Do not include this intro material in your actual manuscript file, but in the body of the email.

2. In a second paragraph of 100-150 words in your submission email, please provide a summary of your entry—what the chapter title is, whether your chapter is a short story, novel excerpt, collection of poems, essay, etc. Who, what, when, and where it is about? How many words and how many manuscript pages? Stand-alone pieces only need one title, however, a collection of titled short pieces, needs a separate Chapter Title for the collection. Resist adding material just to max out our guidelines: 15 strong poems are more likely to be chosen over 25 poems that include 10 half-baked ones. If the work (or any part of it) has been previously published, please be sure to include a citation in this summary.

3. Prepare your chapter entry as a separate Word or Pages file our editors can work with. Use your author name spelled out as one word for the filename (eg: JaneSmith.docx). Include the Author Name as you want it to appear on the very first line, followed by the Chapter Title on the second line, then a single spaced line before your chapter text begins. Include any supplemental material such as endnotes, a bibliography, maps, or photographs (if color they will print in B&W) if your entry calls for them. Do not include anything else in your entry file that isn't actually part of the chapter entry text itself (do not include your bio or summary paragraphs here). Attach the entry file to your email.

We have separate editors for fiction, nonfiction, and poetry. Songwriting entries are edited by the Poetry Editor. Playwriting entries are edited by the Fiction Editor. We expect the ten writers chosen to be announced early in the New Year of 2027 and the collection published later that fall. For more recent information regarding this and our other titles, visit *www.tenpiscataqua.com/writers*

Patrons

With gratitude we recognize these patrons for their generous support of a publication for discovering and celebrating excellence in regional writing

MARTHA FULLER CLARK
TVC SYSTEMS
LINDA & CATHY
BOB & KAREN GRAHAM
PAUL WELCH
MICHAEL STONE
SUSAN DENENBERG
CHERYL KIMBALL